PETER GONDA

DRINKING
AND DRIVING
IN CHECHNYA

periscope
www.periscopebooks.co.uk

Drinking and Driving in Chechnya

First published in Great Britain in 2015 by

Periscope
An imprint of Garnet Publishing Limited
8 Southern Court, South Street
Reading RG1 4QS

www.periscopebooks.co.uk
www.facebook.com/periscopebooks
www.twitter.com/periscopebooks
www.instagram.com/periscope_books
www.pinterest.com/periscope

1   2   3   4   5   6   7   8   9   10

ISBN 9781859641057

A CIP catalogue record for this book is available from the British Library.

This book has been typeset using Periscope UK, a font created specially for this imprint.

Typeset by Samantha Barden
Jacket design by James Nunn: www.jamesnunn.co.uk

Printed and bound in the UK by TJ International

PROLOGUE

What is this fucking guy staring at? Does he know something? What could he possibly know? A short pause, then the anger came rushing back. *You don't know much of anything, do you, my backwoods comrade? Get back to your shack, then, I've work to do here!*

Such were the thoughts that so preoccupied Leonid that he overflowed the jerrycan, splashing petrol onto his boots. He heard the spillage, yet kept his eyes locked onto the curious face of the filling station's owner for several moments longer. He only looked down and readjusted the nozzle after spilling enough to properly immolate himself. Of course, he was smoking, too.

'Only a Muscovite would waste so much petrol! I knew it!'

Leonid just stared at him. *I thought I told you to fuck off!*

'So where are you off to?' the proprietor continued, moving closer. 'The only Muscovites I see around here these days are in uniform.'

Leonid finally deigned to answer the rube: 'We're trying to catch up with the 103rd Armoured Division. Have they been this way?'

'How could I miss them! Such a rumbling … You're with the army too? I suppose you're not going to pay me either, right? You'll … what did he say … *requisition*. Yes?'

Leonid was about to interject, but the old man was already beside himself.

'You bastards are worse than the Mafiya by a factor of three! At least they don't pour my fuel into the soil and expect it to come out of my pocket!'

He turned and was headed halfway back to the shop (where a bottle of vodka awaited him beneath the register) before Leonid bothered to assuage his concerns. 'Relax, old man. Calm yourself. Of course we will pay. Now tell me, how long ago was it that the 103rd came through here?'

'They were here about a day, day and a half ago.'

Leonid walked around to the front of the truck and rapped against the fogged-over passenger-side window. Receiving no response, he jerked open the door violently. Out tumbled Spaska, his forever-benighted partner. Spaska remained unconscious, splayed out on the wet ground, as Leonid grabbed a jerrycan and let loose two splashing gulps of petrol over Spaska's head. He had little respect for those who could not hold their drink. Sometimes, he had to admit, he had little respect for himself as well.

'Crazy, these Muscovites!' This time the proprietor made it all the way inside the shop and found his cherished bottle.

Spaska finally came to. He pulled himself up off the ground, adjusted his bleary eyes, shook the dampness from his long hair and found his Zippo and a cigarette. He prepared to light up, but Leonid gently crushed the smoke against Spaska's face with the palm of his hand – although not before picturing him doing the herky-jerky all ablaze. Losing Spaska might be problematic with regard to the journey ahead. *It is certain that Spaska must end in such fashion ... but why not put it off if one can ... He does sometimes prove himself useful.*

'What the fuck, man!?' Spaska sputtered.

'Load the petrol in the back. Hurry up. We're at least a day behind them.'

'So what? We'll catch them when we catch them.'

'We have the choice to either catch them here and now or later, and at the front. Tell me, Spaska, which sounds preferable?'

'I'll load the back.'

Leonid surveyed the dreary Russian countryside. The Caucasus Mountains were a persistent mirage, far off in the distance – just the way he liked them. The last delivery had seen them lost up there. A bad place, he'd decided, to be lost in, and he'd been lost in enough places to be able to judge the difference. Hamburg, for example, was not a bad place to lose oneself in. Even if you spoke no German and ended up far from the Reeperbahn in some deserted residential area with no bars to speak of, not such a bad place. Especially if you had a pretty girl by your side. (But no, now he was thinking of her again; Leonid forced reality back in and ended the dream.)

In the Caucasus, however, even when you knew where you were and where you were going, somehow you were still always lost. Perhaps it hadn't always been that way. Maybe the war had had a damning effect on the region. Leonid couldn't know, he'd never been there before the war. Why would he have been? There was no money to be made up there back then. Not like now.

Spaska struggled to fit the last of the jerrycans into a large metal container bolted to the truck's floor. Outside of the container, all the remaining space was occupied from floor to ceiling with unmarked white cases, without an inch to spare in any direction. Inside the cases was the vodka.

The owner of the filling station, having fortified himself with a glassful of similar product, came back out to make damn well sure these two paid their bill in full, spillage included.

'Hey, old man, come here and help.'

Together with the proprietor, Spaska finally managed to squeeze the last can in next to the others. He pulled out another smoke, offered one to the old man and lit them both. Yet he did not burst into flame. Leonid remarked on this with some amusement. *You can only cheat death so many times, my little Spaska.*

'Why are you two hoarding petrol? Is there something I should know?'

Spaska laughed. 'Don't go raising your prices so soon. We have to prepare for our return. You may be the last station before Chechnya.'

Tell him everything, Spaska! Everything!

'Ahhh. And why such thick metal for your container?'

'Idiot!' Spaska hit the owner's forehead with his palm. 'If a bullet were to reach those cans, where would we be then, me and Leo, huh?'

Spaska had the habit of mimicking Leonid's manner of speech and syntax whenever he felt he was in a position to lord it over another, an occasion that seldom presented itself – and usually out in the countryside, at that. Still, it irritated Leonid to no end.

'Leo, did you hear what this bumpkin just asked me?'

'Yes, yes, I did. The very same question you yourself asked *me* the first time I brought you on a run! Now pay that hick and get in the fucking truck!" As he said this, Leonid threw his cigarette at Spaska, hitting his coat. Again, no explosion. Now he was infuriated, but managed to calm himself by recalling an old Russian insult usually reserved for women: *Long in hair, short in brains.*

❋

Barrelling down the two-lane motorway at full speed, Leonid took another swig of vodka.

'*Nostrovya!*' Spaska called out, before taking a hit off his own bottle. They each held one. Why not, when the stuff was free-flowing! Leonid felt better now than at the filling station. He'd had at least ten ounces, and even Spaska's constant irritating salutations could not penetrate the cloudy comfort that enveloped him – that elusive cloud, which existed only ever for brief episodes.

It had been roughly nine hours since they had pulled out of the filling station. Leonid was trying to calculate the amount of time it would take the beat-up old truck, going at full throttle, to overtake an armoured division with a lead of no less than thirty hours. He scratched his balls pensively. They were not going to catch up before reaching the front, he told himself.

Unsatisfied with this initial, pessimistic conclusion, he revised some of the variables with greater precision, most of these falling on the convoy's side of the equation, and took another swig to conquer his prevailing defeatist attitude. He recalculated again, until the problem stood in his mind more like this: how long will it take *me*, driving at top speed, to overtake a *Russian* armoured division with a thirty-hour head start on its *reluctant* way to the field of battle?

The answer came quickly enough. Seventy-three minutes later, they spotted a grey and white camouflaged truck pulling a heavy-artillery cannon over a rise about a quarter of a kilometre ahead.

How like a toy it seems. Dragged over a mound by the hand of a child.

Leonid and Spaska exchanged grins, clinked bottles and each took a long pull. It was time for work.

Leonid raced wildly into the oncoming lane beside the column, honking the horn for attention. Spaska, brandishing his bottle, leaned far out the window, joyously pouring the precious fluid onto the muddied asphalt below, implying the massive quantities stocked within the truck. He cried out to the soldiers, shouting nationalistic, anti-Muslim, pro-alcoholism tripe: 'Vodka for everyone, comrades!'

And: 'We'll drink to the death of all Chechen scum!'

And: 'Mother Russia shall prevail against these fucking Muslims!'

And so on, and so forth. Spaska shouted the slogans that almost five months' worth of bloody uphill battle had caused the soldiers' leaders to somehow stop reiterating. No longer was anyone left to prop these boys up. Their predecessors had been sacrificed, and soon, they knew, they would be too. As the vodka truck progressed up the line, a marked difference could be noted in the previously gloomy-faced soldiers. They began to look relieved. A shaft of light had broken through the grey.

Yes, they knew, dimly, perhaps, but they *knew* what kind of hell they were approaching, and the closer they got to it the more their thirst called out to them. That call for vodka, the 'little water', that thing without which nothing on this planet can survive ... it was now within their reach, and their faces, all of them, brightened.

Upon witnessing this hugely spiritual moment, seeing hope enter these men's eyes, truck after tank after truck after tank, Leonid's countenance brightened too. Even if only for an instant, but it did brighten. It always brightened when the smell of currency overwhelmed his olfaction. For he knew, at such moments, that he was closing in on the dream.

❖

Parked on the motorway's shoulder at the head of the column entire, Leonid and Spaska made brisk business. The soldiers were queued up as far as the eye could see – a sea of drunks all the way to the horizon.

Some unfortunates, who had already exhausted their pay during a pre-clash blowout, ran urgently up and down the queue in search of someone, anyone, willing to lend a few *kopeks*. It didn't matter much, however: the truck was emptied in under an hour, with several dozens of boys still waiting. Still wanting.

A general, two-star, approached Leonid. Everything in his manner betrayed his own wants. 'Surely there's more!'

Leonid loathed army brass; his father had made Captain and had never let Leonid forget it. Leonid, as a result, hadn't. 'No, that's the last of it.'

'Another truck ...?'

Leonid shook his head limply.

'That's right. No more vodka! No more!' Spaska yelled out into the crowd from the back of the truck.

'Shut up, you idiot!' the general hissed. 'You're going to cause a riot!'

Then the general turned again to Leonid and implored: 'Don't you have a reserve stash? Something?'

'Ahh, the special reserves. I know now, of what you speak. But it's very expensive for these bottles. Fifteen US dollars per.'

'Are you mad!?'

'For you, only ten dollars.'

'And how about if I just confiscate your truck and everything in it!'

'Comrade, my connections would be very upset.'

The general reddened. 'Fuck your connections! Do you know who I am? Who are these "connections", tell me!'

Calmly, Leonid produced a notebook and pen from his coat and chuckled. 'Well, you know, connections ... everybody has them. Now please, give me your name. Perhaps my connections will recognize your connections. Please, go on.'

Amongst the soldiers now, small altercations were erupting between the haves and have-nots. This was not lost on the general. 'Alright, alright! Ten dollars. Here's twenty. Quickly now, pass me two bottles.'

'The once-great, once-feared Red Army!' Leonid yelled as he pulled away from the column. 'If the Chechens only knew ...'

Spaska laughed beside him. 'Who says they don't?'

'Did you put aside a case like I told you?'

'Of course.' Spaska pulled it out from underneath his seat. He opened two bottles and handed one to Leonid. '*Nostrovya!*'

'*Nostrovya!*' Leonid called back. He was in good spirits now. He had his back to the war. He had the money. He felt safe. In that moment, he even looked at Spaska with some affection. He had lived to see another day, and he had profited.

What his higher-ups had failed to divulge to him – to them, after all, he was nothing more than an errand boy – was the ironic source of the hijacked vodka. It had been part and parcel of a government-subsidized allotment earmarked for a military base outside Georgia. They were selling army vodka back to the army, and at premium prices, too.

Back in Moscow, the bigshots might have had a good laugh over the change-up they had pulled, but the little guys, the men like Leonid who did their bidding, had no idea they were engaged in raping their own country. They were simply worker ants under the thumb of these new Russians.

What Leonid could not have known then, and would not discover until some months later, was that he, with his deliveries, was nothing more than a pawn. And pawns are easily – and frequently – sacrificed.

BOOK ONE
RUSSIA

And you, Russia of mine – are not you also speeding like a troika which naught can overtake? Is not the road smoking beneath your wheels, and the spectators, struck with the portent, halting to wonder whether you be not a thunderbolt launched from heaven? What does this awe-inspiring progress of yours foretell? What is the unknown force which lies within your mysterious steeds? Surely the winds themselves must abide in their manes, and every vein in their bodies be an ear stretched to catch the celestial message which bids them, with iron-girded breasts, and hooves which barely touch the earth as they gallop, fly forward on a mission of God? Whither then are you speeding, O Russia of mine? Whither? Answer me!

From *Dead Souls* (1842), by Nikolai Gogol
Translated from the Russian by D. J. Hogarth

ONE

Leonid opened the door clumsily to the squalid flat he shared with his father. The television was running; slumped in the chair before it was the old man, snoring. *Good*, thought his son.

Leonid stumbled inside and clapped his hands loudly together. His father did not stir. He then went straight to the kitchen and yanked down the oven door with a crash, putting a finger to his lips to shush himself and peering back into the front room. His father slept on. Leonid took note of the unfinished bottle and the loaf of black bread on his father's TV tray, and staggered over to them. Hovering above his father with a sneer, he took a swig of the vodka to freshen himself up a bit and followed it with some fortifying bread to coat and protect his stomach lining. He pointed an accusatory finger at his dear old papa, but made no vocal accusations.

Then he remembered.

You are lucky I still have business with the appliance, old man!

Leonid went back into the kitchen and collapsed beside the open oven. Another swig and he threw himself into it, head and arms. He began to shake the thing violently, as though something was stuck inside it; his feet found no traction on the linoleum floor, and he skidded about helplessly. An encrusted pan fell off the stovetop and bounced off his back. Leonid continued shaking, ever more ferociously, until something unsnapped.

'Aha! You son of a bitch! I got you!'

'What the hell are you doing!? Go suicide elsewhere! Jump in the river! You interrupt my programme, filthy pig!' called the old man from his chair, glaring at his son's ass.

Startled, Leonid withdrew his head from the oven and looked at his father with caution. 'It's just a rat. Don't worry, I've strangled the dirty breath out of him. Go back to your show now.'

'It's all rats now! Rats and pigs!' He turned back to the television.

Leonid remained frozen in that awkward position, waiting. A few moments passed and then suddenly, as though a 'pause' button had been pressed and released, the snoring recommenced. Carefully, he brought his arms out. In his hands, he held the false metal backing he had jerry-rigged to the interior of the oven. He laid it gently against a cupboard and reached into the lining of his coat, to a secret pocket, pulling out wads of various currencies that he threw onto the door of the oven. Leaning back inside, he stacked the booty neatly in a space between the original inner back wall and the false backing. Then he snapped the *faux* wall back into place. Leonid was exhausted and sweaty. The job all done, and being already so close to a horizontal surface, he splayed himself out on the cold kitchen floor and soon joined his father in a symphony of sinus music.

They never used the oven, Leo and his father, didn't even know any recipes that called for one. They were strictly stovetop cooks. Oven-cooked meals had been his mother's domain. Leonid only realized this years after her demise, when the money began to pile up and he needed a hiding place. It came to him on a night two years back when he was preparing a *shchi* for them both: the money would be safe back there. Not from the thieves or hoodlums who dominated much of Moscow of late, not even from the police. No, there it would be safe from the old man.

❁

Shakily, Leonid made his way towards The Royal Majestic Tea Lounge, the main hangout for the organization that employed him. It was one of the largest organizations of its kind in all of Russia, and had far-reaching arms with dealings in Colombia, Israel, Nigeria, Australia, most of Europe and even in the United States itself. They had gone global well before 'globalization' became such a common byword in the language of business. To be sure, they'd laid down their contacts while the Iron Curtain was still up. At least that's what Leo read in the papers, not without some sense of pride. But what he actually knew of this Mafiya of which he was a part was very, very little. He knew only about the dealings he was involved in directly, and even then he only knew his own role, not the whole play.

The question of veracity in the newspapers' claims of existing Mafiya connections in the US interested Leo profoundly. His great dream – unoriginal though it was – was to live in America. Every rouble, dollar and mark he had socked away in his father's oven was to be saved towards that goal. He, unlike his peers, wore no expensive jewellery, did not dress extravagantly, drove no Mercedes and never,

ever threw money away on women. He saved and saved. His only vice: drink. His only virtue: frugality.

The club was nearly empty at this early hour, and Leonid spotted his boss easily. As he approached Miki, who was seated in his usual booth at the Royal Majestic, all this was running through his brain. He was here to report on the last foray into Chechnya, but could think only about America.

'So you made it back in one piece yet again! What did I tell you, these Chechens are as harmless as babies. Have a seat.'

'Good to see you, Miki.'

'So tell me, it went well? No problems?'

'There was an old Communist, a general. He tried to start some bullshit with me ...'

'So how did it end?'

'Not well ... for him! His men nearly mutinied when they realized we didn't have enough for everyone. Let's just say he became distracted.'

'Ha! Sometimes, only some of the time, I become nostalgic for my days in the army.'

Leonid ignored this. The implosion of his head seemed, to him, imminent.

'What's wrong? You look jaundiced! Maybe it's time for a drink, eh?' With this, Miki signalled the waiter.

'No, please. I really overdid it this last time. You know how nervous it makes me, going there. I think I've developed an ulcer. And driving with that fucking idiot Spaska doesn't help, either!'

'Listen, I keep telling you, you're a truck driver, Spaska's a truck driver. It's not as if we have hundreds like you.' The waiter, having arrived with a bottle of iced Finlandia, began to fill two glasses liberally. Leonid watched as the viscous liquid slid down the slope of his glass and slowly collected at the bottom. Then he pushed it away.

'A beer, then. Surely you won't refuse a beer!'

Leonid gave him the nod: yes.

'Bring us two Baltika Extras as well. No glasses.'

From his jacket pocket, Miki produced a bottle of pills and slid it across the table to Leo. 'Drink your medicine and take two of those with it.'

'What are they?'

'Old trick. Vitamins. Just eat them.'

Leonid examined one of the pills. 'How did they get the vitamins into this little thing? We were told to eat our potatoes for vitamins, or occasionally an orange or an apple.'

'They're vitamin B12 pills, from the West. You eat two of these a day and you'll never have to look at a potato again. Now swallow them down with some vodka.'

Leonid obeyed and then made to pass the pills back, but Miki lifted his hands.

'Keep them. You need them more than me, And they're not easy to come by.'

Leonid thanked him.

'Just remember, take two every night before bed. You'll never have problems with hangovers again.'

'Still ... Miki ... Can't you find me something other than this Chechnya run? I think Spaska finally has it down. He can take a new guy out with him, and ...'

Leo, Leo, please, *stop*. You were just complaining about him to me only a minute ago.'

Leonid drank a mouthful of vodka after all. 'I exaggerate too much, that's my problem. I tell you, he's ready. Miki, remember what I asked you? About America?'

'Impossible, Leo. Impossible.'

'But I just read in the paper …'

'How many times have I told you? How many!? The papers are all bullshit! They're state-controlled, just as they were before. It's the same gang of lying Communists! I wouldn't trust their weather reports! We are a small group of businessmen. How should we have operations in America? Do you think I would send shipments into a shithole like Chechnya if I had dealings with Americans? Last time I'm repeating this: in America, nothing! Zero!'

Leonid drank dejectedly from his glass and finished it just as the beers arrived. He had no more arguments. Miki regarded him sympathetically.

'How's the war hero? How's your father?'

Leonid drained a third of the Baltika before answering: 'Still an asshole.'

'Leo, Leo, Leo. I'll tell you what, take some time, two weeks. Take care of yourself. When you're better rested, I have a very important shipment that only you can do. Take care of this for me, and I promise I'll find you something more comfortable. What do you think?'

'That would be tremendous. Thank you, Miki.'

'But understand! This is the last time I will do such a favour. That E55 business was already too much. Two times is too much, eh?'

Leonid got the drift, sure enough. He'd held out his hand before. One more time and it was likely to be chopped off.

'Of course. I understand. Thank you.'

'In the future, try to move slower, you'll go further. If you run, people will laugh.'

Leonid nodded. The proverb was one used with great frequency by his grandfather in reference to his own son's ambitions. Here it meant something else entirely, but it reminded Leo once again that he was more his grandfather's son than his father's. He rose to leave.

'Leo, aren't you forgetting something?'

'Oh, of course.' Leonid pulled a thick bundle out from his coat's secret pocket and handed it over.

Miki tore off the plastic and fondled the two piles of currency. One American, the other German. The roubles Leonid and Spaska could keep a percentage of, but the hard currency was always Miki's.

To his knowledge, anyhow.

●

The favour of which Miki had spoken, Leonid's initiation into the organization, had taken place somewhere between Dresden and Prague – 'twixt the Devil and the deep blue sea. The E55, that stretch of motorway linking these two cities, and specifically the Czech side, was known to drivers throughout Europe for one thing only – sex. A dark nickname began to spread amongst truck drivers, perhaps the E55's most frequent users: 'The Highway of Cheap Love'. It was, in fact, a major motorway converted into the world's largest whorehouse. For miles, one ran the gauntlet of cheap sex.

The girls themselves were mostly refugees from the Balkans or the Caucasus, poor Eastern European women looking Westward but falling just short. Or abductees. Take your pick. They all had one thing in common: they were not there by choice. Known as 'Natashas', they were as good as slaves.

Leonid had been state-trained as a truck driver and mechanic. Then the state crumbled. Spare parts for trucks began to run out, and afterward the petrol stopped flowing, but there was hardly anything left to transport by then anyway, save the vodka. Always the vodka.

After all this, Leonid – along with the vast majority of his former fellow Soviets – started to fret. He began to scramble for work, and three days later he was in a full-blown panic. After the dissolution of the USSR, Leonid – who had grown up with the spectre of complete nuclear devastation – saw himself as being not unlike the survivor of a nuclear holocaust. Better to have been vaporized. Anything but this. The survivors, he thought, were the ones who got it in the ass.

And then, just as all seemed lost, the men arrived. They came to him, not vice versa. He had tried to find them, to find anyone who could aid his cause, but the harder he looked, the more cleverly did they hide themselves. The more he asked after them, the less he heard back. But they had heard everything; they had an ear to the ground. An ear, in fact, to rival those of many intelligence agencies the whole world wide. They heard that in Moscow, there was a truck driver and mechanic, a stout, burly bastard with a bug up his ass, who was in the grip of financial desperation. He fit a very specific bill. And so they came, and no sooner had they come then he was off to that stretch of guilty asphalt between Dresden and Prague.

Leonid shot out of bed, awakened by a loud noise. His father, he was sure. Many months earlier, his father, during a late-night sojourn to the toilet, had tilted a little too far to the right while urinating and had fallen sideways into the tub, smacking his head against the tiles. Leonid had found him lying there awkwardly, one foot dangling over the rim of the toilet, dangerously close to the yellowed waterline. His father remained still.

Leonid had left him there, going instead to sit in the kitchen in front of a vodka bottle. He poured out a tall one, having already pronounced himself an orphan. *I'll call the morgue tomorrow. He'll hold until then. It's funny how many people encounter death in the loo.* His mind followed this idea of toilet fatalities in Russia, and he wondered if the situation was the same in America. Then he imagined what a thing an American toilet must be, an American *bathroom*. How sparkling white the porcelain. He saw pink and blue tiles and shiny golden fixtures, and on the sides of the mirrors, glowing white bulbs, the kind starlets always had for doing their make-up before a Broadway show.

A strange, low moan had entered his reverie just then, and his mind had flashed on a bathtub overflowing with red water. His mother's scarred and nearly lifeless face appeared before him. And the long, deep gashes that ran from wrist to elbow.

His father's moaning turned to grunting, and Leonid lost the image. He returned to the toilet. His father's arms and legs moved crab-like in the struggle to stand upright.

'What are you fucking looking at! Come here and grab my arm, oaf!'

'What's the big rush? I'm coming.'

Leo had reached in, taken an arm and hoisted him up. His father stood, seething, right foot ankle-deep in the toilet bowl, warmed by his own piss. Leonid flushed and the bowl emptied, but his father was still there. *Poor plumbing*, he thought.

Now, once again, Leonid made his way down the hallway, his hopes heightening as he approached the kitchen. He daydreamed about dressing the fresh corpse in women's clothing and propping it up on a bench at the bus stop across the street for all the neighbours to see and mock. He reached for the door to the toilet and opened it. Alas, it was empty.

Next, Leo checked his father's room. Opening the door just a crack, he heard the disappointing sound of snoring. He returned to the kitchen, all his hopes dashed, and opened a bottle. It was 5 AM. He pondered the sharp noise that had awoken him, but could not account for it. These phantom sounds had been plaguing him in recent weeks. Leo took a long pull of the bottle, and recapped it.

Back in bed he drifted off quickly, wishing he were an orphan.

Every so often when Leonid was in town, he would get together with a friend of his, an old truck-driving acquaintance named Piotr, and take him out to a restaurant. Piotr was not doing nearly as well for himself and his family as Leonid was, and in fact was in awe of him. When they met, Leonid tended – uncharacteristically – to go on and on, speaking of his big plans and of how he would soon escape to America. He simply thought of Piotr as a friend who would do as friends do, care about him and support his dreams. Between them lay no walls, no barbed wire, no minefields, no bullshit.

Indeed, Piotr would always listen attentively, but from where he sat things looked quite different. Yes, he would absorb all that Leonid had to tell him, half-enraptured with visions but half-delirious with envy. So there *were* walls and barbed wire and minefields. Because he knew that although Leonid's talk was all quite feasible for him, it never would be for Piotr; moreover, he could never have dined in those special restaurants were it not for Leonid. Therefore, Piotr despised his friend.

The capitalist propaganda machine held both these suckers firmly in its grip, the one believing that Paradise existed and was worth saving for and the other needing and feeding hungrily off the belief of the first.

Before any serious boozing began, Leonid would insist on treating his friend and comrade (so to speak) to a first-class meal, almost invariably a Pizza Hut affair. One had recently opened up in Moscow, and the queues were notorious. Piotr, playing at being the bigger man, would patiently wait in them alone for two hours, allowing Leonid the luxury of arriving only a few minutes before a table opened up. On occasion, however, the queue lasted quite a bit longer, yet Leo was always prepared to pass the time. He had his flask to see him through, should the need arise. Too, as a Russian of the old Soviet school, it was deep in his blood to wait in such a fashion, often in queues that had led to nothing much at all. But these were Pizza Hut queues, and they led, in Leonid's mind, to a place beyond Heaven.

To truly understand, one must first take into account the absence, in Russia then, of anything resembling a decent pizza. Sure, there were admirable attempts, but the main ingredients were always unavailable and substituted instead with items better suited to stewing or pickling. Results were always shoddy at best. Moreover, it was commonly reckoned that one could put nearly any kind of topping on a pie. There were souls who would disgrace a slice with offerings such as an unpeeled potato wedge, or the tail end of a herring. The lofty notion of *choice* prevailed. Yes, they all had choice now, choices that had been withheld for several generations. Choice was everywhere. The people had spoken, and their choice was pizza.

But the battle was on to see who could afford it. Not everyone had this thing, *choice*. Certainly Piotr did not, and despite his best efforts to shield him from this knowledge, all Leonid actually managed to do was push his face in it.

Despite all this, when the pizza arrived, they each dug in with greed and lust, one with wrath, the other with envy and both, certainly, with gluttony. (Neither man with sloth, though, nor with anything resembling pride.)

When it was all over, their shirtfronts were impeccably stained, and as they walked the streets of Moscow afterwards, smoking Cuban cigars, their chests puffed out. They had the look of the canary-eating cat in their eyes, and were admired by all who had never known what it was to become engorged with American-style pizza. Yes, all bowed before them. All save those disposed to cleanliness, who were absolutely fucking appalled.

'I wonder,' thought Leonid aloud, 'if the pizza is as good in America …'

'Of course not! It's even better!' Piotr became belligerent. 'Pizza Hut is a great American institution! Russia will always turn greatness into shit!'

'But Americans control this one.'

'They are on Russian soil, no? They were corrupted the minute their airplane landed!'

Leonid thought about this. It seemed to make sense. 'So you really think the pizza will be better over there?'

'By far, my friend! You will see when you are there. I promise this!' Piotr glanced over at his inebriated mate. 'Perhaps you'll even send over a slice so that I, and my family, can truly understand what a pizza could and should be.'

'Piotr, I will send for you. For you and your family. This is not a life for you – for us.'

Piotr searched Leonid's face suspiciously. He looked long and then he looked hard as Leonid, unawares, swigged from his flask and looked ahead. Piotr could not detect the lie he so dearly wished for, the hint of which would give him the excuse to throttle Leonid. But it wasn't there. Frustrated, he grabbed the flask from Leo's lips and had himself a taste.

'So, Leo, tell me of your father. Is he still thriving?'

Piotr always did know where to land a punch.

Two

Leonid's balls had been handed to him by his father soon after his mother's death. His father before him had had his balls handed to him in Afghanistan by the *Mujahideen*. As for his father's father, well, Stalin had tried to hand him his, but death had handed Stalin his own first.

Leonid's father had been sent to war at the age of thirty-nine, as a tank commander. His wife was already showing signs of depression, and had not wanted him to go. Leo was just fourteen and still loved his father. He, too, begged the man to stay. It would all be over in a month or two, his father assured them.

The war would slowly reveal itself to last, not months, but years. A full decade thrown over a cliff. And soon after it, the dissolution of the Soviet Union came. And soon after *that*, the slow undoing of Leonid himself. These things take time.

His father's own undoing came early in the conflict, on a cold and windy day in November 1980. His tank had broken ranks on account of conditions beyond the control of the crew, and found itself trapped in a ravine surrounded by *Mujahideen* bunker positions. Heavy fighting ensued, and just when one of the boys fired off a money shot at a *Mujahideen* bunker, an enemy fighter in turn fired a rocket-propelled grenade at the tank from the exact opposite direction. The RPG beat the tank's projectile by nanoseconds. The outcome was significant. The two missiles collided head-on, in an explosion mere inches from the tank's gun. The concussive effect on the crew was devastating. The effect on the gunner was most impressive: he took the brunt of the explosion, and was eviscerated.

When Leo's father was returned to his family, they could not recognize him, although his injuries were psychological in nature rather than physical. His behaviour had changed completely. Whereas he had once been robust, talkative and humorous, now he was transformed into a caved-in, sardonic old grouch. He spent his entire time sitting in front of the television, bottle in hand. Every so often he would grunt out a demand.

'Food!' he would call out, and his weeping wife would prepare something for him in the oven. He would never complain about or fuss over what sort of food was brought him. It was all just fuel, nothing more.

On one of the rare occasions that his father was not in front of the television, Leonid's mother decided to have a look by herself. When she turned it on, no image came, just a threatening buzzing sound. She backed away cautiously; had she not, she would have been killed. Instead, when the television (made at the Rubin factory in Moscow) exploded, fragments from the screen embedded themselves in her face.

Her husband's reaction to this was, first, to send Leonid out to buy a new set. Next, seeing his wife's new visage upon her return from the hospital, he laughingly labelled her 'Scarface'.

Now when he required something from the kitchen, it would be: 'You there, *Amerikanski* gangster, food! Hurry up, Scarface!' Always this gave him pleasure, her less so. She fell into an abysmal depression after the incident, crying constantly and avoiding all reflective surfaces. Leonid tried to soothe her nerves, but she was inconsolable. She was so far gone that after a short while, even her husband's crude remarks hardly got through to her. She didn't care anymore. About anything.

❁

His father's utterances eventually grew longer. They were not just food requests, but brief critical analyses of the economic, political or social situations splayed out before him on the TV. 'Dog fuck dog!' he would often remark: a catch-all phrase that summed up his entire philosophy.

He delighted especially in the quick succession of Soviet leaders from 1982–85. Brezhnev died first. 'The shit that sent me to that fucking hole! Fuck him!' (Then he would stare coldly at Leonid, as though it had been Leo's fault that Brezhnev was his namesake. As though he had named himself.)

Next came Andropov, who had tried to stymie the flow of vodka through Russia's veins. 'Filthy reforming abolitionist pussy! Go back into your mother's cunt!'

He was followed by Chernenko, who didn't even live long enough for anyone to commit his name to memory. 'Another corpse! They're dropping like flies!'

And then came Gorbachev. He looked fit enough. No one expected him to die, although six years later, most of Russia would wish he had done.

✿

After his mother's untimely death, Leo was immediately thrust into her role. He had hardly begun mourning her than the job of executing her wifely duties was upon him, the very same duties he believed had killed her. His father mourned not at all. His only acknowledgement was an echo of his comments on Chernenko's passing: 'Dropped like a fly!'

Flies don't kill themselves, you fucking asshole, Leonid would think, while washing plates.

His father seemed at once more and less content with the new change. One less annoyance, yet, at the same time, one less person to look after his needs. To be sure, there would be no more incessant crying and, from now on too, a certain complicity between father and son would underlie all consumption of alcohol. A new balance had been struck. Neither would benefit.

Leonid and his father went through the motions just as an old married couple might, all emotions muted, one always sensing the other's needs and wants, patiently absorbing the other's trite and tired comments and insults; the other always just being the other. Their relationship, then, was one-sided, exactly as they both wanted it. At least, how Leonid wanted it. He was quite satisfied that he didn't need a damn thing, not an iota of love, affection or any of their byproducts, from the old bastard. His father, on the other hand, was permanently out on that call, though a slight smirk would occasionally escape his stony countenance, suggesting that he was not adverse to their arrangement.

This is not to say, of course, that Leonid had no use for his father. He did. So what if the old man never knew, or even if he did know and pretended not to? He still served a purpose, and the purpose was this: as he lay in front of the television, dead drunk to its pessimistic observations on worldly affairs, his son would add his own hysterical accountings. But Leonid's propaganda was quite different from the state's. His spoke specifically of, and to, the plight of the individual. Specifically and individually, to Leonid's. He'd kvetch all night long into his father's dozing ears.

In the early days, he would shout: 'Where in the fuck are the blessed truck parts!?' Later, he would scream into his father's dreaming ears on other subjects, as the USSR began to sink even further. 'Fucking Gorbachev!' Months later, it would be, 'That Yeltsin is a cunting drunk!' washed back with a water glass that never held any water. Only ever vodka.

Then, at last, the refrain changed to: 'Fucking Miki, why does he refuse to help me reach America?'

In the West, there existed a thing known as a suicide hotline, whereby you could call up at any time during the night and deprive some inept agent of compassion of his rightful sleep, bedevilling him with all your problems. In a Russia devoid of such compassionate innovation, this was how Leo's father served him best: as a non-feeling punching bag.

Still, now and again, in the middle of one of Leonid's lamentations, his father would suddenly be roused from sleep or delirium, jump out of his chair and make one of his own proclamations apropos of nothing much at all: 'Really, now – those Chinese are going too far!' Then he would storm out of the room. This ruined things on Leonid's end, and would send him into a depressive funk. Had he no one to talk with? Was no one listening?

Thus, not through any unity with other put-upon people, not through any rising together against the corrupt and bureaucratic Soviet state, but only through self-interest did the one-time benevolent idea of communism collapse, if slowly; these things take time.

The failing of communism was the same failing of parental guidance that Leonid endured as a result of his father's neglect of his own responsibilities. Like a sculptor who had never taken hold of anything but impure materials, Leonid's father had left those in his care as nothing more than misshapen clumps.

❂

Leonid's responsibilities on the E55 included a new role. He was now a hybrid of driver and pimp – *pimp*, of course, to the girls' *whore*. He protected them from abusive customers, doled out smack, made sure to keep the girls a bit strung out and secured all their revenue. But he also did their laundry, cooked their food and listened to their woes. On occasion, he would drive them to an abortion clinic. He was thus also *chambermaid* and *transport engineer* in addition to to his status as pimp. He was trained in this multifaceted job by a friendly enough fellow named Vlatsky, and shared it with him.

'Here we deal in human *biznes*,' Vlatsky told him. 'You, like me, are a truck driver by trade, but now driving the truck is the least of our responsibilities. These girls, they are *chelovecheskoye zoloto*: human gold. You must always treat them as such. Never think of them as mere whores. To us, they are gold.'

The girls operated out of a tractor-trailer. Tarps were hung on wires to create 'bedrooms', and each of these had a single dirty mattress on the floor. There were twelve such rooms in the trailer.

Vlatsky had Leo, as his underling, clean the bedsheets every so often – but not nearly ever enough. This meant a two-mile walk down the road to the Czech town of Dubí for the use of its laundromat. Leonid was never the only one performing this chore. There would be the regular washerwomen, and then there would also be tens of other large bastards queued up behind them, chatting, all waiting to wash their own girls' sheets.

At the end of every two weeks, upon the arrival of a replacement crew, Leo had to drive the eighteen-wheeler back into Prague. There he would unload the girls at the mother whorehouse for freshening up and working the urban crowd, and then hand all monies over to Bronski, the Russian boss in charge of Prague and the surrounding areas. Bronski would calculate Leo's five percent and hand it over; Leonid then had a week off.

Aspects of this employment did upset him. Some he got over, became used to over time. Others, he found harder to swallow. He knew, for example, that as shitty as the situation was for his girls, circumstances were far, far shittier for the girls belonging to others along the road. And it still irked him, after eleven months of the same routine, that Vlatsky had not once done a load of washing.

Despite the job's setbacks, it did have one major drawing point for Leo: it never impinged on his vodka intake. And he, for his part, never stopped intaking.

The young French musician rose from the table where he was holding court and crossed the nightclub in search of the toilet. As he pushed against the door with the appropriate pictograph – unmistakable, as a huge cock had been inked onto it – an unfamiliar arm slipped under his. It was the bouncer.

'Toilet no good,' he offered up in the Queen's English. 'Broken; you follow me, yes?'

Not waiting for a reply, he pulled the uncomprehending Frenchman down a corridor, opened an emergency exit and thrust him out into an alley. The Frenchman got the point, but still lamented the days of yore when all Russians of any consequence spoke his own tongue.

Relieving himself against a dumpster, he was surprised by a barrage of quick, hard rabbit punches to his kidneys, followed by an elbow to the temple. Dropping to his knees and propping himself up against a wall with one hand, he tried to regain his footing. But his assailant knew his business well, and was now working the ribcage in with the heel of his boot.

Finally, prone on the pavement, damming up a rivulet of his own urine, the musician was left alone to ponder the meaning of things.

From his table inside, Leonid watched respectfully as Miki, large and smiling, returned to his friends in the opposite booth. Removing a pair of brass knuckles, he said loudly: 'No more interviews for the laureate tonight.'

The combined laughter from the five Mafiya tables roared above the club's balalaika music.

The Frenchman, Hugues Boyard, was a minor celebrity in his native land but an absolute unknown in Russia, so he had been completely taken aback when the director of an organization that called itself *Russia/France Inter* contacted him. The Russian people would be honoured were the great man to accept an invitation to enrich them with his music on a grand concert tour of their country, he was told. They would handle all the bookings, and five buses with drivers would be supplied to transport him, his band, crew and all their equipment across Europe and into the great Russian expanse, he was told. The opening concert was to take place at Moscow's renowned Bolshoi Theatre. This, too, he was told. He had agreed to everything, of course, and immediately.

Everything went swimmingly until the caravan reached the Polish frontier. Words were exchanged between the Russian drivers and the customs officials. Loud, threatening words. One of the Poles went so far as to draw his gun. Hugues, watching the scene from his seat, remarked that the guards were repeatedly pointing at the lower cargo holds of the buses. He then remarked that money was changing hands. Once underway again, he questioned his driver, but found the replies severely wanting.

At the next rest stop, Hugues stormed over to the holds and opened them himself. One after another, they teemed with pharmaceutical merchandise.

●

In Moscow, on the eve of his gig at a venue markedly less prestigious than the Bolshoi, Hugues had sat, seething, in the green room of a television studio. The Bolshoi concert might have been a fiction, as was the promise of touring the country, but the invitation to appear on Russia's most-watched entertainment programme had not been. There was to be but one show in a local dive known more for cage-fighting matches than jazz fusion, and Hugues was to promote it. He'd felt used. He'd felt stupid. And worst of all, he'd felt humiliated, an emotion known to drive many men to commit acts that can only be described as appallingly idiotic.

A production assistant then knocked on the door and led Hugues to the soundstage.

Leonid and his father were having their dinner in front of the television when Hugues was introduced to all of Moscow during a segment near the end of the programme. An attractive young woman was conducting the interview, and had she understood a word of the replies her questions were prompting, she most likely would have fled the country post-haste. Had she been of a more diligent bent, and had worn the earpiece given her, things might have turned out slightly better for her; anything is better than being slain atop the shitter. But, as she told her producer time and again: 'I don't care what they're saying! No one does! People watch to see me, not them! Me, and my big pair of new tits!' Thus her reaction to each of Hugues's comments had been to smile and thrust said plastic orbs flirtatiously under his nose.

The Franco–Russian interpreter was paid to speak quickly and translate live on the air. First, Russian into French, and then vice versa. He was not necessarily concerned with what was being said, so he said all, and all had been broadcast instantly.

Some of the Frenchman's juicier quotes included:

'Perhaps your country would be less of a black hole if every little aspect of it wasn't controlled by a bunch of corrupt oligarchs and their fucking Mafiya.'

And: 'It's recently been reported in France that three in every four Mafiya-type thugs are homosexual, and that half that number are HIV-positive.'

And: 'Quite frankly, your gay little Mafiya can kiss my French ass!'

And then, to the hostess: 'Where shall we meet after the show, you horny little tart?'

Meanwhile, over at his place, Leonid patiently absorbed his father's exclamations, jeremiads and insults. He'd never seen the old man like this before. Now jubilant, now mournful. Sometimes screaming in a rage, other times choking on his own laughter.

'He's got it right, this Frenchman! You and your friends are nothing but a pack of homos! If Brezhnev knew the state Russia is in, in the hands of eunuchs, he'd never stop puking! He's your namesake, you know! How did it come to this? How? Did you hear what he said? Kiss his ass! Har! That's good! Was a time the French were scared to death of us! Now look. Oh no! Now that French scum is going to defile this Russian goddess from the TV! We're all being raped! What are you, anyway? What kind of son are you!? You idiot! Get out of my sight! God help me, I'll squash you like an insect!'

Somehow, the Frenchman had loosened the whole gamut of his father's emotions at once. Leonid could only wonder what the effect had been on other households. Had this scathing portrayal of modern Russia, with its organized crime and oligarchs, stirred the turds as Hugues had wished it to? He couldn't say. He did know one thing: how his cohorts were likely to react.

React they did. First, they made sure that Hugues and his friends would, that very night, find themselves enjoying free drinks at the Royal Majestic, get the little prick on their own turf. They even arranged, for the group's entertainment, a Lenin impersonator – one of hundreds plaguing Moscow's nightclubs. Later, they would take care of the show's hostess in the harshest and most demeaning of fashions. She, the media as a whole, should have been fully aware by now just how serious was the offence.

As for Hugues, he was (clearly) not one to lie down and accept being treated shabbily, not live on air and not on this night, either. He managed, after several minutes, to regain his composure and rise to his feet. The fire exit locked to him, he tramped through the alley and back out to the street in front of the Royal Majestic. The bouncer grinned knowingly and waved him back into the club. Hugues glanced at him, hatred seething in his irises. A severe expression to be sure, and one that elicited little more from the bouncer than a sad, resigned shake of the head.

Hugues approached his band's table, ignoring the guffaws emanating from the Mafiya section. 'Where've you been so long? ... And what the fuck happened to your clothes!?'

'Does anyone have a weapon?'

His bandmates shrugged in unison.

'A fucking weapon! Anything! The Mafiya is here tonight. They saw the show. I'm going to teach them something!'

'Don't be a fool! You've avenged yourself, now let it go.' This from a musician wiser than Hugues. But his counsel was rendered useless by the appearance on the table of a penknife attached to the house keys to some Parisian dump. Hugues unfolded the two-inch blade and beheld the thing as if it were Excalibur itself. A waitress passed close to him and he grabbed her, holding the knife to her throat.

'Who the fuck was it!?' Hugues screamed above the din, advancing on the Mafiya tables. 'Which of you pederasts was it out in the alley, eh? Quickly now, before I give this Ruskoff slut a facelift!'

The French table, fearing the worst, slid their asses down low in their vinyl-covered seats. The Mafiya tables, however, reacted quite differently. They stood up and drew guns, and their laughter, well, that only increased. One wit even made light of the blade's size in proportion to his own member, a joke that forced some of his companions to drop to their knees, laughing.

The whole scene fizzled to nothing more than a humorous anecdote when an undercover policeman deftly disarmed the Frenchman, bowed deferentially to the Mafiya tables and escorted Hugues and his friends out of the club. Once outside he scolded them severely, informed them that their lives were in great danger and that they would be deported back to France immediately.

Back in the club, laughter and general merriment reigned through the night on all sides except for Leonid, who found himself shocked by the Frenchman's quick descent into the most desperate and foolish kind of violence – and this from an artist, the most sensitive of classes! His head shook, or he shook his head – he couldn't tell anymore. He drank again, vodka upon vodka. Something was wrong, terribly amiss, and it was only just now revealing itself to him.

All around him was nothing but laughter.

In the days that followed, Leonid found himself reaching more than he ever had before, for *something* – for what, exactly, he could not discern. It was blind groping for something familiar in a lonely darkness. He stretched his mind this way and that, trying to remember, going further and further back into the past. This went on for several days, until finally something did come. It wasn't much, but Leonid felt there was some meaning behind it: a memory of a walk in the woods with his grandfather. What could have happened in those woods? He thought harder, and then he thought some more. The feeling that something had been gleaned or taught during that walk was all he could muster.

In the days that followed, as much as he struggled with it, the recollection stood resolutely as just that: a walk in the woods, and nothing else. Something would not reveal itself to him. *I will ask the old man what he can tell me about Grandfather.* This he told himself, and left it for another time.

❂

Here he was again now, summoned by Miki, at the door of the Royal Majestic. Leonid found himself looking forward to the meeting, which surprised him. Normally he'd be loath to attend, nervous and nauseous, thinking of Chechnya and imagining the worst, enduring all the symptoms of fear. Only drink could steel his nerves.

Yet this time he was eager for a mission, a purpose, something to do. Introspection, after several intense days, had become the thing most dreaded. It had ousted war and even death from the throne. He had never felt so alone, so lost and in such a vast darkness. Clearly, it didn't agree with him.

He was ripe for a vodka run into Chechnya.

He sat across from Miki in the usual booth. There was a bottle of Smirnoff on the table, and Miki wasted no time in pouring out a glass for Leonid.

'Are you not taking those pills I gave you?'

'Of course, Miki. Why do you ask?'

'Because you look like shit! Look at the bags under your eyes! You're as white as a ghost.'

This was news to Leonid. 'Really?' It seemed to him an improvement over jaundice. 'I suppose I haven't been sleeping very well.'

'Why not? I'm wondering whether or not I should even send you on this next job.'

'I'm fine, really. I'm ready to go back. That thing with the French guy threw me off a bit. That's all.' Leonid lit up a smoke. 'It affected me.'

Miki could not believe what he was hearing. 'That stupid little shit!? You're still thinking of him?!'

'I was a little surprised by his actions. And those of others.'

'Which "others"? Whom are you talking about?'

Leonid was reluctant to say more, but Miki's eyes persuaded him that silence would not be acceptable. 'My father's, the guys', yours.'

'This, I can't believe!'

'Why should you care what some stupid foreigner says on television? It makes no difference to us, to what we do!'

'You are quite mistaken, my dear, naïve friend Leo. It's a question of national pride. What do you imagine the French would do to a Russian who spoke that way about them in their own country? Trust me when I tell you that your friend got off easy with a little beating. Very easy!'

'And the reporter? What about her!?'

'Don't even mention that cunt to me!' Miki turned away in disgust. 'She, more than anyone, should have known not to fuck with us.' He went on to explain that she'd been warned sufficiently in the past regarding the production of a series of Mafiya exposés. The way Miki enunciated several words heavily and with pregnant meaning, specifically the word 'sufficiently', was not lost on Leonid. He began to drift. Several disconcerting images conjured by the implications of that 'sufficient' warning flashed through his mind. He was taken aback at having recognized Miki in a few of them. Leonid looked back at Miki, and found his boss searching his eyes in such a fashion that he had to look away again.

'You're soft, my friend, too soft for this work. You don't understand how business works. You have to develop a killer instinct, or you'll never move ahead in this world.'

Leonid shook off these comments, smiling at no one in particular. 'There's a book, maybe you should read it,' Miki continued.

'What! A book?' Now he was laughing outright.

'Don't be so quick to mock. I read it, too. It's a very intelligent book.'

'What's it called, this book?'

'Ah, that's the question. Let me remember ... Vladimir! What was that book you lent me?'

A tall, wiry man turned from his conversation with the bartender. 'It was called *The Seven Effective Addictions of Supremely Wealthy Persons*, something like that.'

'That's right, that's it. I remember the way it was described below the title: *Lessons to Change Powerless Personalities*. Leo, you should go find a copy. This is a book for you. It'll help you through this depression you're going through.'

'Who's depressed?'

'I'm serious, Leonid! Where's the old tough guy I used to know? I need him back for this job. It's no joke!'

'He's still here, Miki. Sitting right in front of you.'

'Look at me when you fucking say that!'

This command almost threw Leo from his chair. Miki had never spoken to him like this before. But then an old anger flooded back. *Fuck you, Miki! You don't talk to me like that, you fucking potato farmer!* He looked straight into Miki's eyes. 'I'm right here in front of you. You don't need to worry about me. I do the job you give me. Always.'

This seemed to satisfy Miki. 'Good. Let's have a drink.'

He refilled both their glasses. They each drained them in one go, neither man breaking eye contact.

THREE

One slow Monday morning, a man with a pronounced limp approached Leonid and asked him in German if any Muslim girls were available. Leonid, still soused from a busy Sunday night on the E55, paused for a moment. He didn't speak a word of German. All he could think to do was call out to Vlatsky, who was asleep in the truck's cab. When Vlatsky finally arrived, pulling his clothes on, Leonid simply pointed to the man, said 'German' and staggered towards the cab in search of a comfortable place to have his blackout.

'What do you need?' asked Vlatsky in German.

'I'm looking for a Muslim slut. Do you have any?'

'I have a Muslim girl, yes.'

'So where is she? Let's see her.'

Halfway up into the cab, Leonid called out: 'What does he want?'

Vlatsky told him, and he suddenly took an interest. He remembered Galina. He'd seen the scars on her back, but had never asked about them. Knowing she had escaped from Bosnia was enough to tell you most of the story. Leonid stared at the man for several seconds and decided that he didn't like him. *What do you want with a Muslim, you sorry little gimp?*

'Why should the girl be Muslim? Tell me that.'

This confused Vlatsky. 'Why should she be anything? You've heard these perverts' requests before. If *you* want to figure out the "*whys*", then be my guest. Me, I have no time for that. I'm going for Galina.'

'Ask him the fuck why! What happened to your "human gold"?' This took Vlatsky aback. He thought about it for a short moment.

The German-speaker now revealed himself to be, in fact, Serbian, and understood every bit of Russian spoken in front of him. 'Listen to your friend, comrade,' he said. 'Why? Why is the sky blue? Who cares! They turn me on, you satisfied? Now come on and show me the bitch. I'll pay double.'

Vlatsky decided it was fine, a done deal, but added: 'My girls are not "bitches". Please refer to them as "ladies" in the future.'

Maybe Vlatsky was right. Maybe they both were. Just another deviant. Leonid had seen all kinds of fetishes in his time out here, things he could never have imagined before. Why not a Muslim fetish? Still, he followed as Vlatsky led the man to where Galina was and pointed her out. They observed her from some distance, sitting at a picnic table and drinking coffee. In reality, she was much further away from them than they realized, lost in contemplation, adrift in another time and place.

'Where's she from?' asked the Serb.

'She came from the war. From Bosnia.'

'Perfect!' cried the Serb. Then he switched tongues and called out to her in what must have been Serbo-Croatian, because she shot straight up. He approached her slowly, still speaking the language. Leonid thought he recognized some place names – 'Srebrenica', 'Goražde', 'Sarajevo' – coming out of the man's mouth. Galina started to shake, worse even then she would shake during a withdrawal. Tears began streaming down her face, and soon after, urine started to course down her legs. The Serb leered before her now, enjoying the spectacle. He grabbed her hand and led it to his erect member. She shrieked. Then he shrieked too. Vlatsky had given him a well-placed kick to the back of his balls. The Serb went down heavily.

'Are you all right?' Leonid asked Galina as he went to her and held her. 'What did he say to you?' She couldn't stop shaking.

'You know her, asshole? Huh?' Vlatsky ribkicked the blubbering war criminal.

Leonid led Galina towards the tractor-trailer, trying to soothe her. This he did awkwardly, not having tried it since before his mother's death. As usual, vodka was the answer. He offered her his flask, but she needed something stronger. Something with a hell of a lot more kick. He helped her up the ramp and past some action going on behind one of the tarps. She sat down on a mattress. He drew the tarp closed and offered her the vodka once again.

'I need the shot. Please. Quickly.' She said this as she tied her arm off with a belt.

He did not argue. She reminded him of Dresden, of the girl he was trying so hard to forget. Removing the supplies from his inside pocket, he emptied the contents of a small packet onto a spoon and added water. Holding his lighter under the spoon, he began to cook. Leonid sucked the concoction up into a syringe, and then administered the shot of heroin. It was, after all, part of his job.

❂

All the plans had been laid for Miki's birthday party by his guys. The dumplings, sausages, sturgeon, caviar, cakes and pastries, strippers and pre-paid prostitutes, assorted drugs and even pizzas had been arranged in the preceding days and weeks. As had the *pièce de résistance*, Moscow's most revered Lenin impersonator, who had a talent for singing and dancing as well as making overblown speeches. Falling smack in between New Year's and Orthodox Christmas, Miki's parties were always grandiose. Even so, this year was going to be his biggest yet, and the party was to be held in no less prominent a venue than the Royal Majestic Tea Lounge.

The day after this feast, Leonid, with Spaska beside him, would be leaving yet again for Chechnya, with little time for anything but sobering up before hitting the road. This, of course, would not be the manner in which they used that time.

Everyone came that night: former KGB, current FSB, Russian film stars, politicians, random wealthy people. Should any of the invited be too old or decrepit, or should they be deceased, then their middle-aged children would be duty-bound to put in a respectful appearance. Dues were owed, and where Miki was concerned they were seldom overlooked or forgotten.

Naturally, all Miki's boys were there too, some from as far off as Italy or Xinjiang Province in China. Some came from even further abroad. Some came from America.

Even Borzoi was there that night, and he rarely ever reared his flabby head in public. Not lately, not anymore. His name was known to the media. He was wanted in many countries, by many men. In America, Canada, Israel, Colombia and most European nations (save Italy, Serbia and Bulgaria), he would certainly have been picked up by the authorities. Russia was not exactly pleased with him, either. Clearly, he had accomplished much, if recklessly. On his neck, above the collar line, he had a tattoo – and not a traditional Mafiya tattoo, with a meaning known only to a select few members. No, this was a Borzoi original, and its meaning was clear to everyone who saw it: a visceral depiction of a fist smashing through glass. Borzoi, naturally, being the fist; everyone else, the glass. It was said of him that he was truly safe in one place only, and that place was Chechnya. The exact town was never mentioned, if known. And if known, never mentioned.

Of the attending politicians and FSB or ex-KGB officers, none were overjoyed to be seen sharing food, drink, cocaine, sex or even oxygen with Borzoi. Of the three, however, the ex-KGB men were least perturbed by his presence. After all, they had already turned rogue. Still, even though they were fully aware that they fought on the same team as the man now, there was still a certain squeamishness about them. 'Was anyone on to them?' they worried. A knee-jerk reaction, before they remembered that nobody cared anymore.

The politicos were even less sure of themselves, even the drunk ones. They had the same reflexively anxious response as the old guard, though they had a sounder reason for it: the starving Russian majority was screaming after their blood, screaming for a return to the old ways, to the Politburo and the Party. Any hint of post-Soviet state corruption could lead overnight to a storming of the gates.

For his part, Borzoi cherished the pained expressions on the politicians' faces as he shook their hands and posed for flashbulb photographs.

To be sure, this night was not like other nights. To many there, it felt as though Russia might fall in on itself at any moment. The old world with its old words ran up against the new era with its new words, such as the all-important *offshorny schet*, or offshore account. Some older words had developed new and greater relevance than ever. *Khalyava*, for example. Something for nothing. (Another, more colourful interpretation was 'cheap railway station whore'.) And only the Mafiya seemed fluent. It was enough to put anyone on edge.

Over by the buffet table, several elder statesmen were giving a visual how-to of *khalyava* themselves. They filled their plates as well as the deep pockets inside their coats. Virtually anything smaller than a folded-up RPG could be hidden in these coats, which were specially ordered from tailors around Moscow to precise specifications. The best tailors, the cleverest, even lined the pockets with thick plastic, so that certain mealtime acquisitions such as sturgeon or lobster tail would not ruin them. It had become expected behaviour of Russian elites to pocket whatever was on offer at these kinds of grand affairs. No one blinked anymore. It was considered rude to object to this pocket-stuffing. Borzoi, of course, cared little for such social conventions and, spying a bottle of American bourbon disappear under the Deputy Minister of Agriculture's armpit, he loudly announced: 'Just like old times, eh, Mikhail Simonovich!'

The Deputy Minister shrugged and looked awkwardly around the room to see who had heard or seen.

'You can't fuck the whole world, my friend!' laughed Borzoi.

Around the buffet, people began to snicker.

Regaining his composure, the Deputy Minister rejoined: 'Why not? Always remember the old Soviet proverb – what's yours is mine, and what's mine is … mine!'

The room broke out in laughter. Everyone clinked glasses, made a toast to Miki and had another shot. They laughed, and remembered to forget.

❂

Early in the evening, Leonid and Spaska were introduced to one of Miki's associates from America, a character named Andrei Lvovich Trofimov. Leonid was immediately taken with him, and invited him to sit in their booth. Andrei accepted coolly. To Leonid and Spaska, it seemed that his every move was performed coolly. He was James Bond to them. This made Leonid feel self-conscious; the way he dressed and spoke, he felt, were beneath this Russo–American Adonis. When Leonid summoned a waiter and asked Andrei what he was drinking, he half-expected to hear the classic Bond drink order. It didn't come. He was still Russian, after all: 'Double vodka, no ice.'

Leonid and Spaska both parroted the order. Normally, they'd simply order a bottle. Leonid wanted to hear about America, and wasted no time in getting to the point.

'So where do you work, Andrei Lvovich?'

'All over. But I live in Coney Island.'

'An island! What do you say to that, Spaska? Not bad, eh?'

'Nice. Very nice. Is it in Hawaii?'

Andrei was far too polite to mock them. 'It's not actually an island. It's in Brooklyn. In New York.'

'Even better. Can I offer you a cigarette?' Leonid pulled out a pack from his jacket. Spaska did the same.

'Thank you, but I don't smoke.'

'You're right. A filthy habit. I'm in the process of quitting, myself.' Leonid put his smokes away. Spaska lit one up.

'So how about yourselves? Where are you working for the organization? Here in Moscow?'

Leonid was embarrassed to say, Spaska less so: 'We work out of Chechnya.'

'Chechnya! You work under Borzoi, then?'

'No, no, we work for Miki.'

'Ah, the birthday boy.'

Leonid, red as *borscht*, changed the subject. 'Can I ask, Andrei Lvovich, how did you come to work in New York?'

'Of course. My uncle. He was kicked out of Russia in the Seventies and started up the business in America. When the Wall came down, he sent for me.'

'Ah, one of the first, yes?'

'That's right. He's a real old-timer.'

'Listen, I've been trying to get a foothold over there, but it's proving very difficult. Do you think you could put in a –'

Andrei stopped him short and handed him a card. 'Call me at this number and we'll see what is possible. Now, please excuse me, I see that I'm being called over to Miki's table. Good to meet you.'

With that, Andrei rose and went over to the bigshots' table. Leonid stared at the card for several seconds before being interrupted by Spaska: 'Let me see, too.'

'Shut up. It's of no concern to you.'

'But since when are you thinking of going to America? You never told me anything about it …'

'Shut up,' I said. Leonid watched as Andrei shook hands with Borzoi, Miki and the others.

'No contacts in America, eh, Miki?' he muttered under his breath. 'Nothing? Zero?' Then he smiled and put the card in his breast pocket.

❁

Borzoi pushed the Lenin impersonator up to Miki's table and screamed into his ear. He wanted, demanded, a pitch-perfect recreation of a speech by Lenin to the Extraordinary Seventh Congress of the Russian Communist Party in 1918, in which he had referred to the external enemies of the new Soviet Union, and how they were tearing pieces off her. Borzoi had a strong sense of irony, and felt it was perfect for the moment at hand, as perfect as two or three things can be together at once: 'As perfect as herring, black bread and vodka!' he yelled.

Impressively, the impersonator managed to stumble through the speech, drunk as he was. The man was clearly more than qualified for his job. Most in his line would have been left clueless as to the details of that particular speech. Certainly, he deserved a tip. The spectators erupted into applause as he belched out the summation. Miki pulled him onto the table enthusiastically, knocking half the wind out of the poor bastard. They ordered more rounds, and for every one the table downed, the Lenin was compelled, by Borzoi, to down three.

Leonid observed all this from his table in the corner. The underling table. A table of nobodies whom nobody noticed. They cared not, however. Not when they knew they were still doing fifty times better than the hordes outside. In one hand, Leonid held a slice of Pizza Hut's finest with chomp marks in it. The other held a half-sizer of Stoli. Spaska, beside him, said: 'There's sure to be some mischief with that Lenin down there, I'll bet. I've heard stories of how Borzoi can be.'

Leonid told him to shut up for the umpteenth time that night, and kept watching Miki's table. The party raged on, but not without some early exits. And not without fear.

❉

Leonid and Spaska were still there after the more distinguished guests had left with pockets full of delicacies and whores on their arms. For them, as well as for all the other Mafiya types, to leave before Miki would have been a sin, a sign of disrespect and disloyalty. It was unheard of. Even if Miki was too far gone to remember, someone else might – and you didn't want anyone getting a leg up on you. Not ever.

Leonid surveyed his table and became full on the measure of his own loyalty and respect. Sure, all the crew had stayed, but he alone remained awake – if just barely.

He needed a piss, and felt he deserved one.

Leonid stepped over the unconscious Lenin, lying on the floor below four barstools pushed too closely together. He had a chuckle over that, and continued on towards the lavatory. Before most people had cleared out, the Lenin had made those stools his early and unsteady bed for the night. Obviously, it had not worked out as well as a booth might have done. Leonid did not remark on the fact that the Lenin's feet had been bound together with duct tape. He staggered onward, passing Miki and Borzoi sitting at the bar, still drinking, still coherent, involved in a whispered conversation. *Real generals!* thought Leonid. *They are stronger than all of us combined.*

The two generals were discussing something in great depth, yet they noticed Leonid as he drew near, and noted that he had observed their discussion. Miki asked Borzoi a question. Borzoi nodded 'yes' in reply, and looked at Leonid with undisguised contempt. Like a throwaway object, like nothing. He said: '_____ will look after him.'

Leonid shrugged and smiled stupidly. He had overheard something, a name mentioned, perhaps a Chechen name but he couldn't be sure. He was over-the-rainbow drunk now. All he knew was that the thought filled him with a sense of well-being. That someone would look after him; he liked that.

General Borzoi smiled back, pointed at him and said: 'See you soon, Comrade Fuckface!'

He laughed. Then Leonid laughed. Then, finally, Miki's countenance fell in with the other two. They all laughed for what seemed to Leonid an hour. They laughed long after there was anything worth laughing about.

Leonid woke with a start about thirty minutes later. A stall door had slammed. He found himself atop a toilet, refocused his eyes and made quick survey. His trousers and underwear were around his ankles. That was good, he thought; but then he realized how cold his ass was He turned to find that the wooden seat was up in a vertical position behind his back. Between him and the Devil lay only a few short inches of porcelain. He took a breath and looked between his legs, straight into the bowl. Thankfully, nothing but yellowed water.

He wondered what day it was, and how long he'd been there. Loud cheering from beyond unnerved him. He was still unsure of himself, still intoxicated. He pulled himself together, drew his trousers up, exited the stall and threw some water on his face. A second wave of fanatical, bloodthirsty howling came at him. He left the toilets behind slowly, with a caution unknown to him since childhood.

Under the emerging redness (for the Royal Majestic was swathed in reds of many hues) he stepped out into the great hall, the sound now deafening. He saw a crowd before him, cheering, clapping, some even snarling. For a brief instant he thought it was all for him. The moment chilled him to the bone. He could not guess the meaning of this spectacle. *Do they honour me in this way? Do they accuse?* Such thoughts clouded his mind until he picked out an individual directing an unfriendly gesture of Italian provenance above Leonid's shoulder. Another pointed an accusatory and more precisely aimed finger several feet over, to Leonid's left, stirring him from his delusion.

He took several steps into the crowd and turned towards the source of the pointing. The chanting behind him now, he witnessed something that could be said to encapsulate the entire Russian genome, from prehistoric barbarity to Peter the Great to Orthodox iconography, all the way up to the Bolshevik murder of the Romanovs, the Stalinist murder of the masses and KGB torture techniques, finally ending at the fall of the Berlin Wall, all of it reeking of vodka consumed and regurgitated.

Leonid watched, along with several dozen other henchmen, as Borzoi, aided by two thickset, barrel-chested goons, crucified the Lenin to a post at the bar. Having been merciful enough to avoid the use of nails, Borzoi instead employed copious amounts of duct tape to achieve his goal: his gift to Miki on the occasion of his birthday.

The Lenin was beside himself in drunken righteousness. 'Lenin is deserving of your wrath!' he wailed to the bawling crowd. A thrown bottle of Baltika Classic broke against his skull. 'I deserve this!' he cried before passing out as his remaining arm was lashed to another pole. Borzoi hopped down from the bar and threw a glass of cold water into the Lenin's face, which briefly revived him. Blood and water commingled on his brow, and for an instant he seemed lifelike again.

Borzoi bowed towards Miki, proclaiming: 'Even better than the one in the mausoleum!'

Miki bowed back in appreciation. Borzoi had outdone himself, and Miki would grant him his request. Of this, Borzoi was sure.

'Please, I implore you, just kill me.' This from the cross, from the Second Coming-to.

Then Borzoi said the words aloud. He gave breadth and depth to an expression that would reverberate with Leonid long into the future: Borzoi reached up, gave the Lenin several little avuncular cheek slaps and smiled. 'Don't worry,' he said, 'you will not die. You'll see!'

Three hours later, Leonid and Spaska stumbled out of a taxi in the southern suburbs of Moscow in front of a large parking garage. They approached the keymaster, who knew them well; despite their condition, he walked them towards a truck and placed a key into Leonid's palm. Leading them around to the rear of the vehicle, he opened up the back to show them, by way of confirmation, all the crated vodka. Leonid nodded vaguely. The man cut a box open by way of further confirmation, to show that the vodka was indeed inside. Spaska reached for a bottle but Leonid slapped his hand away.

'Fine,' he said to the man as he closed the back of the truck. 'We'll be on our way, then.' Having proved his diligence, the keymaster walked off, shaking his head.

Leonid was about to start up the truck when he noticed an envelope taped to the dash in front of Spaska.

'What's that?'

Spaska had already passed out. Leonid shrugged the letter off, ignited the engine and pulled out of the garage. Two minutes later, he hit his first red light. By the time the light turned green, he was unconscious.

❂

Leonid came back to himself around two-thirty in the afternoon. Spaska was still out, and the truck was exerting gentle pressure against a tree on the pavement. The police had driven by this scene several times that day. The police weren't interested.

Putting the truck in park, Leonid stepped out. Several minutes went by before he could be sure where he was, exactly. Not in terms of which street, but which city. This he achieved by asking wary passers-by.

Getting back into the truck, he threw it into reverse and got himself level with the street again. Once righted and prepared to take his southerly course, he spotted that envelope on the dash as if for the first time. Last night was lost to him forever.

He opened it and read the short missive. It was from Miki and it simply read: *Call me before you enter Chechnya. Don't forget!*

That was a trifle odd; Miki had never before asked to be contacted. Still, Leonid said to himself: 'You want to chat, we'll chat.' He left it at that. Sometimes the biggest warnings come to us in little ways, ignored until too late and understood only in hindsight. And that was just the path that Leonid was about to take.

He made his way through the sprawling outskirts of the city, getting lost several times and then finding his way again. It was impossible driving there. The street names were being changed on a frequent basis of late, back to what they had been called in pre-Soviet days. Some had been renamed completely after poets, writers and dissidents who had gone forever missing in the gulags, whose names could not have been uttered until a few years earlier. Onward he drove, past old buildings being torn down and new ones going up, without anything resembling urban planning and certainly without a thought to the needs or wants of the populace.

Was it any wonder that no one could get their bearings anymore, when the building you were searching for on Heroes of Stalingrad Street was now a pile of rubble on Akhmatova Street?

There was still more to this problem. In the Soviet era, many of the city and regional maps to which the public had access had been falsified. The Communist Party believed it was protecting itself from espionage and insurrection. All it actually managed to do was keep everyone constantly off-balance. If you opened up a map of, say, St Petersburg, and followed it diligently, you might believe you were three blocks from the Neva River. If you continued and crossed just one street over from where you made this assumption, you might end up *in* the Neva, struggling to get out of your now-submerged vehicle.

So here is Leonid, lost in south Moscow with a bastard of a hangover, his navigator still out for the count, and he has to be in Chechnya in three days. What does he do? He pulls the truck over, dismounts, opens up the back and grabs a few bottles for the ride. As there is no such thing as being 'a little bit lost', he decides to take it to the extreme.

FOUR

Leonid decided against patronizing the same petrol station they had done the last time around. He didn't like to leave traces, and still felt that Spaska had given away too much to the old coot running it. For one so imprudent in his life in general, Leonid managed to take this job seriously. This time he opted for a larger, more anonymous filling station.

It was ridiculous for him to worry like this – nearly everyone was up to something crooked now – but he couldn't shake the feeling that he was about to be caught out around the next corner. By what force, he couldn't answer: God, the Devil, the FSB, a stray Chechen bullet or something worse, he didn't know. He just always felt that trouble lay ahead. Today, for once, his instincts would be correct.

While Spaska took care of filling up the jerrycans, Leonid went off and put through the phone call as Miki had instructed. The bartender at the Royal Majestic summoned Miki to the phone.

Without so much as a 'hello', Miki said: 'You're not in Chechnya yet, are you?'

Leonid told him they were still a ways off.

'OK. We're going to try something different this time.'

'Such as?' Leonid's apprehension grew.

'You're going to make this delivery to the train station inside Grozny. Don't worry, there'll be troops stationed all around it. You'll be safe with them. Now, it's in the town –'

'They're shelling Grozny!'

Miki sighed deeply before continuing, more forcefully: 'They're not shelling themselves, you idiot! The guerrillas are on the run, and the city will be in Russian hands within the week. Now take my instructions down carefully.'

❀

When Spaska got back into the truck, having paid for the fuel, he found Leonid already halfway through a bottle. Wrongly encouraged, he opened one of his own.

'So what did Miki say?'

Leonid refused to answer him. 'None of your damn business!' He felt it wiser that the kid not know until absolutely necessary.

He took the route given to him by Miki and again, after an hour or so, Spaska questioned him. 'Why are we going this way?' But Leonid maintained his sphinx-like demeanour, leaving Spaska to wrestle with the riddle.

A few more hours into the drive, columns of refugees passed them, heading in the opposite direction. Spaska rolled down his window and asked some of them where they were coming from. When he got the answer and heard 'Grozny', he just stared at the side of Leonid's face in disbelief. Leonid kept his eyes on the road.

In Russian, *grozny* translates as 'terrible'. As in, 'Ivan *Grozny*'. Unfortunately for Leonid and Spaska, they were about to discover just how *grozny* Grozny actually was in these *grozny* times: it would turn out, of course, to be a *grozny*, *grozny* mistake.

They pulled up to a Russian checkpoint, and a soldier all in white bade them stop. Leonid could barely distinguish him from the wintry backdrop. He informed the soldier whom he was meeting on the other side, and where. Hearing him, Spaska realized his worst fears were becoming real.

'Oh my God!' he shouted. 'What the fuck are you doing! Are you crazy?'

Leonid could not answer him verbally. He just shook his head. *Your time has run out, my friend.* The whole way down from the petrol station, his thoughts had been with Spaska. As scared as he was himself, he felt quite certain of Spaska's early demise and now feared it would happen before his very eyes. He definitely did not want to see it.

Spaska was off his nut now, screaming at Leonid in a blind rage. Even the soldier's order for him to contain himself could not make him stop. Leonid shook his head again. *Your time has come, my poor idiot.* The more he was able to intuit and hear the fear in Spaska's voice, the more he addressed his partner with sympathy and compassion. In his own head, anyway.

The soldier decided to ignore Spaska, and focused on Leonid. 'What's in the truck?'

'It's an urgent delivery. For the 131st Brigade.'

'How nice. What's in the back of the fucking truck?'

'OK, OK. It's a special delivery for some top generals.'

'I don't give a shit who it's for! What's in the truck?!'

Spaska wailed: 'It's fucking vodka! What else!'

Upon hearing these words, all Leonid's newfound compassion immediately bled out his pores, replaced once more with that old, bitter desire. *I will laugh as you die, my little Spaska. I will die from laughter over your death, you stupid cunt!*

'Get out and open the back!' ordered the soldier. 'Now!'

✸

Leonid counted the soldiers at the checkpoint as he opened the trailer doors. There were eight in all, probably two more out shitting in the woods or smoking crack. That made ten. From this number he deduced that he was about to be 'taxed' three cases. He was wrong. The soldier whistled for two of his comrades, and instructed them to unload eight cases.

At any given checkpoint in any given war or occupation, the same old joke always applies: there is bad news, and then there is worse news. The eight cases of vodka were the bad; the soldier now told Leonid the worse.

'The guys you're looking for, they're in bad shape. Got hit hard this morning. They're stuck in the city centre near the train station.'

✸

As they drove along the main boulevard into Grozny's town centre, Spaska grew still more agitated. They passed several rotting corpses, pieces of them being torn off by starving dogs.

'We're going to die in this shithole! Fuck!'

'Speak for yourself, asshole. We lost eight cases because of your big mouth!'

'Who cares! If you do, if you still care, then you're fucking mad! You're suicidal! Because that's what this is, a suicide mission! It's fucking insane!'

Leonid backhanded him, hard, across the mouth. 'Calm yourself, unless you want another of those. We have to do business soon, and I can't have you carrying on like this when we're doing business. You understand?'

Apparently he did. The smack calmed Spaska down a bit.

'Listen to how quiet it is. You're crying for nothing. Would you cry in front of our soldiers? What would they say upon seeing you, a fucking tourist, acting this way? In a few short hours you'll be leaving! What about those who live here, who have to stay, what would they say? You should die from shame, you big pussy!'

'OK, OK. I think it passed ...'

Leonid ignored him. He ignored the corpses. He ignored the newly feral and rapacious hounds. He ignored the bombed-out buildings on either side of the boulevard. He ignored the far-off, sporadic gunfire. Everything he said to Spaska was directed at himself. It was to his own sanity that he spoke. *Listen to how quiet it is.* His fear was such that he saw nothing but the ten feet of road ahead of him. *I'm a tourist. A few more hours, and I'm gone.* His fear transfixed his thoughts as well as his gaze. Nothing could break through to him now.

It was early evening when they came upon the train station and their objective, the 131st Brigade. Nervous Russian guns were trained on them. Leonid pulled up to the soldiers ever so slowly, without the usual honking. Spaska was half out the window, with his hands in the air by way of surrender.

The men looked haggard. Many were wounded, and Leonid noticed dozens of booted feet sticking out from under a large tarp on the ground. Their leader approached the truck, putting a finger to his lips. 'What are you guys, a pair of crazy people? Do you realize where you are?' he whispered.

'We're here from Moscow, to provide the vodka. Didn't you know we were coming?'

'Not at all – but I won't say no to a drink.'

Leonid found this rather strange. Miki had specifically told him where to find the brigade. He had never done that before. He had also instructed him to give them a 'special price'. And *that* was so far from Miki's character that it should have set off all of Leonid's warning systems. But it hadn't.

News of the shipment spread quickly and silently through the ranks, smiles replacing the hard stares. Queues were formed, and business began. Roubles were traded for bottles.

And that's precisely when the shooting began. The soldiers were aligned like ducks in formation, and the Chechens perched on the rooftops opposite made quick sport of them. The Russians were cut down instantly.

Bullets broke bones and sprayed blood across the train station's façade. RPGs blew tanks and armoured personnel carriers to hunks of twisted, burning metal. Leonid and Spaska ran for their seats and hightailed it out of the shooting gallery. The Chechens, however, had other ideas, and took aim at the truck.

Leonid careened down the street frantically in a full-blown panic, cases of vodka falling out of the still-open trailer doors. 'What the hell are they shooting at *us* for!?' he bellowed.

Spaska was crying now, muttering something about his mother. Their left rear tyre was shot out. Leonid lost control of the vehicle, and smashed head-on into the concrete base

of a street lamp at 90 kilometres an hour. Then everything
went black.

●

When Leonid first came to, his eyes slowly regaining their
focus, he had trouble remembering what had happened. He
knew he was in Grozny. The crash eluded him for the most
part, but not the shooting. Mostly he couldn't remember why
he wasn't dead.

Then he saw the crushed bonnet and cracked windscreen
before him. His first thought was that he'd probably gone too
far with the drinking yet again, and had fallen asleep at the
wheel as he had done before leaving Moscow. But how could
he have done that amidst all the gunfire? Next, he turned
his head slightly to his right and took in Spaska, whose
own head was completely through the windscreen. Blood
from a gash in his neck ran down the length of his body
and spread out across the crumpled bonnet. The blood was
rust-coloured rather than red, but even with that hint, it took
Leonid several minutes to reconstruct what had happened.

It occurred to him that he should examine himself for
wounds in the side-view mirror. He found that he had a deep
cut across his forehead. *Probably the fucking steering wheel.*
The haemorrhage trail had run down between his eyes, and
flowed past either side of his nose. Apparently, after that he
had drunk deep of his own blood, for the trail ended at his
mouth. His teeth were as crimson as a vampire's after a feast.

He looked back over to Spaska. *I fucking knew it! I called
this one months ago!*

He decided that above all else, what he needed was a
shnort. He reached under Spaska's seat with his right arm,

expecting to find their private stash. Nothing. This baffled and annoyed him. He decided to continue the search in the back of the truck. When he reached to open his door, a searing pain ran up his left arm; he understood that it must be fractured. He used his right arm instead, and climbed down to the pavement. He was still too far gone to realize his shoes were missing.

Leonid was beyond disappointed to find his entire haul vanished – including the petrol. There was nothing back there but the smashed glass of the bottles and the soaking cardboard of the boxes that had held them. He went back to the cab and checked under his own seat. Again, no vodka. *This can't be happening.*

Now he noticed the petrol gauge. Empty. *That's impossible!* It could only be due to siphoning, he knew. Everything was tumbling down on him now. In quick succession, he reached for his wallet: gone. He searched Spaska for his: gone. He remarked that Spaska was shoeless, and inspected his own feet: gone were his shoes. Where were their coats? Gone. *This just keeps getting better and fucking better!* He reached for his pack of smokes to find them gone, too. *I'm nothing without these. Nothing!* All that was left was a small box of matches in his trouser pocket. Clearly, the thieves who had taken his cigarettes had little need for a light.

Only now did Leonid start to think about the passage of time. He looked at Spaska's dried, brown blood and finally understood that it meant a great many hours had elapsed since the accident, probably more than twenty-four. Certainly enough time for every scavenging Chechen for miles around to relieve Leonid of something they felt they needed. It was all becoming clear.

'Thieves! Criminals!' he cried out. He tried to picture the lowlifes who would steal the shoes off a dead man. And worse, steal his vodka. He thought again of Spaska, and began to weep. 'Thieving, fucking sons of whores!' he bellowed, and continued crying feverishly.

But the more he tried to fill his mind with poor Spaska and to release bitter tears for him, the more the lack of vodka pervaded his mind. Where in Grozny might he locate some? He knew that a severe withdrawal was upon him, and he knew that this was the real reason for his tears.

'Thieves!' he screamed out again, pointlessly, into the wasted city streets. The thieves couldn't hear him. They were all hiding in their warrens, struggling to survive and hunkering down; soon the Russians would resume their nightly shelling of the capital. Dusk was nearing quickly, and a light snow had begun to fall.

So here was Leonid – shoeless in winter, penniless, bearing a useless arm, without transport or even papers ... and on top of that whole damnable pile, no fucking booze in sight. If he had that one thing, he told himself, he'd be able to cope. He probably could have laughed off the whole debacle. Without it, he was well and truly lost.

He knew that the time was at hand to find shelter, but another idea crept into his desperate, alcoholic head. He climbed up into the trailer and searched out a wet piece of cardboard, examined it, smelled it – and then ate it, followed by a snowball chaser. His logic held that the cardboard would have retained the vodka that had spilled and soaked it. Whether or not his theory would prove true or false, Leonid spent that night in the back of the truck, watching the Russian bombs fall as spectacle and eating cardboard as libation.

✹

He awoke in the morning to find he'd eaten just about all that remained of the boxes. He also found that he had the direst need of a cardboard shit. And then he discovered something else: cardboard shits, in general, are fucking painful.

Quick decisions had to be made now. He surveyed the fresh layer of snow on the ground and knew that if he stayed there, he would succumb to exposure by the following morning, despite the relatively mild January temperature. Search for vodka or shoes. He understood that the odds of obtaining drink in this wasteland were virtually nil. He stuffed his pockets with as much vodka-sodden cardboard as was left. Whilst doing this, he spied a large, pointy shard of broken glass and pocketed it as well, a useful as a weapon if needed – against an enemy, or against himself: either option remained open.

He descended from the trailer and said his last goodbyes to Spaska. Then he stole his erstwhile partner's thick woollen socks, doubling them up over his own.

Thinking of those dead, boot-wearing feet under the tarp, he headed back towards the train station. Not only were the boots and the tarp gone from that place, so too were every other boot, coat and weapon from the freshly dead. There were hundreds of corpses, and Leonid understood the part he had played in their massacre. Again, he cursed the thieves.

He searched the streets for nearly an hour. He found about three to five corpses per city block, but not a one was still in possession of shoes or a coat. *Spaska and I were not the only victims in this department.*

Finally, he came upon a leg with a shoe on the foot. Not a corpse, just the leg. The size appeared to be about correct, and Leonid decided that one shoe was better than none. His bile rose at the thought of laying hands on the thing, but he swallowed hard and got down to it. Not an hour had passed since he'd screamed about others robbing the dead yet here he was, stealing from a mere appendage.

The work of untying this shoe was harder than it seemed at first. The limb had no real weight; the substance it would have had, had it still been attached to its former owner, was absent. The thing would constantly flip over, and as Leonid had but one good arm, he could not hold it in place. All this movement, all this squirming of the inanimate object, reminded Leonid of the very thing he was trying to block out: the idea of handling a blown-off limb, and the insult borne by the act.

In the end, he used his legs to hold down the upper thigh in what must have looked like some kind of wrestling pose, and finally got the bloody shoe off. With it came the odour of dead, mouldy foot, which hit him like a wave – and then out it came. All the remaining cardboard within him, he vomited copiously and painfully onto the leg, furthering the insult.

Ten minutes later he hopped away from the befouled limb with his new shoe tied securely onto his own right foot.

✿

He was still hopping about the city come dusk, with no idea what to do about shelter. He had entered some flats but found them depopulated and stripped bare. Leonid deduced that if the locals had abandoned them, there had to be a good reason, and if they weren't deemed safe by their standards then his search would have to continue.

He came upon a young boy, about ten years of age, carrying a small package. This was the first living person he had seen since he'd come to, and he felt oddly comforted by the kid's nearness, so he followed him at a distance. The child seemed not to notice him, and it was not until he reached a certain spot that he surveyed his surroundings. When he saw Leonid, he stopped cold and stared at him. It appeared as though he was waiting for Leonid to pass, but Leonid would not. He just stood there obstinately, staring back at the kid. After about a minute of this, the kid gave up and crawled through a paneless basement window, revealing his hideout.

Emulating this feat proved a trifle difficult for Leonid. He lowered himself to the ground, got onto his back, turned his legs into the hole and, fearful for his arm, searched with his toes for a foothold. He slid down a little further and deeper but still could not find a perch. Then he went a little too far and dropped the whole way in, his head smacking against the top of the windowpane on the way down, reopening the scab on his forehead. He toppled over upon landing, onto his fractured arm. The scream he let out bounced off the walls of the cavernous room, piercing the ears of its three inhabitants.

The mother and her son and daughter did not mind his intrusion; in fact, they barely seemed to acknowledge his presence. The scream jolted them, but that was all. The mother and daughter went back to their work by the fire they had going, making dinner as if everything was right in the world.

Leonid pulled himself together. 'I am called Leonid. What are your names?' he asked in Russian.

The mother shook her head. Neither she nor the children spoke a word of Russian. She and her daughter, who looked to be around thirteen, both wore headscarves. They were

Chechen Muslims, and people of Leonid's ilk had little knowledge of them. They lived in Russia, as did many others, but they were not Russian. Most of Russia was not Russian, even the Georgian who had tried to artificially homogenize the country by shuffling whole ethnicities around this vast land.

Leonid ass-crawled over to a lonely corner and watched them. He noticed the mother opening the package the boy had brought. It was rice, and she carefully emptied a paltry amount into the pot that the daughter held above the fire.

Where's the husband? Leonid was nervous, lest the man should arrive. An angry, contentious Chechen patriarch was the last thing he wanted to see at this juncture.

The shelling began soon after the rice was prepared. Every blast sent a vibration through Leonid's body that he did not need; his body was already vibrating from within. Withdrawal had set in, and every explosion reverberated hundredfold in him. He ate some of the leftover cardboard from his pockets in the hope of offsetting the sickness.

Meanwhile, the small family took turns eating the rice out of a teacup with their hands. They had only the one cup. The son was about to take a second helping, but his mother stopped him. She filled half a cup, walked over to Leonid with it and held it out to him. In truth, he really couldn't be bothered with food at that moment, but was so moved by the gesture that he could not find it in himself to reject it. He received the cup with his good arm and placed it between his legs.

As he ate, he watched the mother searching through her coal supply for some wooden sticks. She seemed to approve of two, and put them aside. Next, she went to a little bag that Leonid had not noticed before. She pulled out an extra headscarf and tore it in four places: one lengthwise – the longest – and three others, according to width. She collected some mud from the ground, grabbed the sticks and rags and came back towards him.

First, she rubbed the cold mud gently into the skin of his left arm. He just sat there, observing her actions in bewilderment and wincing a little when she touched the fracture point. She determined that it was his ulna that was fractured, and smiled to indicate it was not a bad one. She placed the shorter stick along the inside of his forearm and the longer one along the outside, motioning him to hold them in place. Then she then tied them tightly to his arm in three places, which made him cry out in pain. Finally, the woman concocted a sling out of the longest piece of cloth, and slid his arm into it.

Leonid was amazed. 'Doctor?' he asked. She recognized the word, smiled and shook her head. She then washed all the blood from his face with a damp rag, and cleaned the ugly scab on his forehead. He'd forgotten all about that. *Good Christ! I must look like I've come from beyond the fucking grave!*

When all this was done, she went and lay down between her two children and gazed at the fire. She gestured for Leonid to come closer and be warmed, but he was already sweating with the fire inside him. He shook his head, letting her know in the most primitive way that he was fine where he was.

He watched them fall off into slumber and ate more cardboard, though he could tell by now that that idea was not working out for him. He was in for a bad one.

Outside, the bombs were coming faster and harder. A cacophony of explosions. Inside, this scene had played itself out so quietly between these people and himself, a Russian and some Chechens.

Leonid almost slept that night.

Leonid drifted somewhere between sleep and awareness, reality and nightmare. All four intermingled. As he lay there shaking, his body cold with sweat and his thoughts tormenting him, shells exploded outside; he was sure that each and every one had scored a direct hit on his life.

He had visions of his father splashing about in the tub, unable to get out of it, even drowning in it. What would the old coffin-dodger do now that Leonid was gone and lost in this hell? Would he even notice? How would he eat? Who, even, was left to bring him his vodka? He heard his father scream, a soul-scarring bellow, and it went right through his bones. Leonid started fiercely and changed positions, unsure whether he had really heard that scream or if it was part of a dream. Given the circumstances, anything was possible. Might have been someone gunned down out in the street. He couldn't know.

More shells fell, and with the steady thumping he went to sleep again. He saw his mother watching television in the old flat. She turned from it and smiled at Leonid. There was an explosion – either the Russian bombs falling on Grozny, or the Russian-made television that had self-combusted and scarred his mother. There had been a spate of such incidents, and his knowledge of them worked itself into his dream, so that it was now raining TVs in Grozny. A moment later he saw his mother in the bathtub, the water red all around her, as she died. As she killed herself. She said but one word before bleeding out: 'Leave.' And then she was gone forever. Again. He wept quietly.

He next witnessed himself pulling the shoe off a foot, only this time it was Spaska's. Spaska asked him why. He explained that he only had one, and needed another. 'And what of me?' cried Spaska, blood pouring from his mouth. Leonid just shrugged.

Then there was gunfire. He saw the soldiers, all their bits and pieces flying at him. He tried, in disgust, to escape the fleshy assault, but no matter where he hid, the blood and guts found him: under a car, inside a closet, behind his mother.

An abrupt change came suddenly to the dream. He thought of his stove, his precious stove and its contents. What would become of them? All that money! He was sure that his father, the stupid fuck, would attempt to cook, and burn it all, along with himself. Oh God! How did this happen?

His mind flashed on Miki. He remembered the ugly smile Miki had trained on Leonid the night of his party. He convulsed violently, and then Borzoi came to him. His fat, leering face as he crucified the Lenin. Leonid awoke and vomited pure bile onto the cold ground.

When will it stop? 'Make it stop!' he shouted, but again, only in his mind. Everything that came to him that night, believable or fantastical, was really just in his head. The evidence of a life lived, and how. The only thing he or anyone else could ever really call their own.

It was not to his liking.

The following morning did not fare much better for Leonid. He had been boozing hard on a daily basis for months without cessation. Now he would face the consequences.

The mother awoke early to find him a shivering and sweating lump of a thing. She knew what it meant, but was powerless to alleviate any of his suffering. Instead, she tended to what she could. She dismantled the sling and applied more mud to his arm. He wasn't there at that moment – he was reliving Galina's hell back in Bosnia, the way he had imagined it. He could not be reached. Still, the mother continued with the mud treatment and put the sling back on.

Leaving him there, she and her children then climbed out through the window to search. For what, they could not say, exactly – more food, more firewood – just *more*. Of anything.

Hours after their departure, Leonid had a brief reprieve and regained cognizance. He surveyed the room and became despondent upon not finding the family there. *I scared them off. I must have.* He began to think of the mother's situation. *She is widowed, I am certain.* He reasoned out her kindliness towards him. *She was trying to adopt me as the new father to her children. It wouldn't have worked!* He inferred her husband's fate, growing angrier. *He's joined up with the rebels and left his family in this state, the pig! Probably one of the shits who fired upon me! The ones who killed Spaska!*

He went on and on in this vein, until they returned. Upon seeing them, this negative train of thought was quickly silenced. The mother and daughter had come back first. After setting down their pickings – wood and kindling – they began building a fire. Once they had got it going, the mother bade Leonid come closer to its warmth. Although he felt by turns hot and cold, he followed her advice.

After he was resettled, the mother searched through the bundle of sticks they had brought and produced, to Leonid's great amazement, a left shoe. She put it on over his large foot, which took some work; she struggled with it, the shoe being too small by about one size, but she got it on him in the end. Throughout the process Leonid felt he might cry, but fought off any display of emotion.

Moments later, the boy came clambering through the window. He whispered something into his mother's ear. She pointed to Leonid. The boy approached him, and from his trouser pocket produced a miniature airline bottle of whiskey. Leonid nearly went into shock.

The mother took the bottle from her son's hand and knelt down beside Leonid. She held his head like a baby's and put the bottle to his lips. And like a baby, he suckled the alcohol from the midget bottle. Although he knew this would help only a little, and that he would still suffer, he now began to weep openly, and could not stop for several hours. He even turned away the portion of rice that was offered him later in the evening, so overcome was he with tears. He cried as one who had discovered something like truth, to whom truth had always been denied. He cried like the Buddhist dead, reborn into this world of pain instead of moving on. Then he shook with his own thoughts, all the night long, occasionally fingering the shard of glass in his pocket to see if it was still there, to see if it was still real. To see if he still had options.

Like mother, like son.

BOOK TWO
CHECHNYA

O Allah! Who sent down the book ... Who makes the clouds drift ... Who defeats the armies ... Defeats Russia! O All Mighty! O All Powerful! O Allah! Indeed we ask that you scatter their firing, and shake the earth beneath their feet, and strike fear in their hearts. O Allah!

Cripple their limbs and blind their sight, and send upon them an epidemic and calamities. O Allah! Separate their gatherings and scatter their unity, and make their condition severe amongst themselves, and make their plots go against them, and show us in them the amazements of your Power, and make them a lesson for those who do not learn lessons! O Allah! Hurry their destruction, and make their wealth as booty for the Moslems.

From *A Dua [invocation] for the Believer*
www.qoqaz.com (Chechen *Mujahideen* website,
now defunct, 1999–2000)
Translated from the Arabic by: unknown

FIVE

On Leonid's third night of penance, the Good Lord smiled upon him. A man plunged headfirst through the empty window, evading gunfire in the street above. He hit the mud floor with a thud, and immediately started venting.

'Jesus Christ! The feckers tried tae kill me!'

He said this while examining two Nikon cameras for damage. When he was done, he looked around the firelit room and discovered he was not alone. He saw the kids and their mother first, and gave them a low bow. The children giggled, finding him comical. The mother, less so. Then he saw Leonid, and presumed him to be the man of the house.

'English?' he queried. Leonid nodded yes.

'Aces! Listen, pal, I'm totally knackered! I been oot in that shite for two days on the hoof now. D'ye mind if I rest up a bit here with you lot?'

What business of mine is it where you stay! Does this one think I'm King of the Chechens? And where did he learn his English, for God's sake? 'Of course,' Leonid replied, 'no, I do not for mind.'

'Brilliant! Nae meaning tae jump right tae it, but what say we celebrate the union? As I say, I'm completely deid on my feet here, an' …' Here he pulled out a smallish baggie of questionable substance and waved it before Leonid.

'What d'ye say? Have a go at chasin' the dragon?'

Leonid could barely understand the Scotsman's speech. He leaned in and said, simply: 'What in fuck you are talking?'

'Her ... oo ... in,' sang the Scot in his best Lou Reed impersonation. 'C'mon, let's have a go!'

Leonid understood now. He thought back to administering shots to Galina back on the E55, in the back of the truck. He thought of the bliss that would so quickly descend upon her after indulging, and the pain she would be in before the drug did its work. He figured he could fare no worse, and rolled up the sleeve of his right arm with great difficulty.

'What're ye doin' there, pal?'

'Preparing for shoot dragon.'

'No, we'll be *chasin'* this dragon. Nae need fer needles. Just some flame, foil and improvised pipe. Up yer blowhole, yeah.' He pulled out a lighter, some aluminium foil and a ten-pound note.

'I see. Even better. Needles, I do not need.'

'There's the lad,' said this new, strange, sudden arrival. And with that he got to work. He rolled up the note and handed it to Leonid. Next, he packed up the foil with the junk and lit the lighter underneath. 'Suck up that smoke, now. Aye, there's th' ticket.'

Smoke rose off the gummy substance and Leonid chased it as it melted before him. The Scot did Leonid up right before asking: 'What about th' missus, then? She up for a taste as well?'

'Is not my wife, her ...' Leonid was already forgetting the words for 'pain' and 'despair'.

'I see. Liberated couple, is it then, ya dancer?' The Scot motioned for the mother to have a go. She turned away. He shrugged, and then did himself while Leonid tried to imagine how dancing came into it.

Leonid would suffer no more, not from booze withdrawal, nor hunger, nor any other earthly craving. He just lay there in complete and delightful stupefaction. His bound arm, his situation, it all meant nothing now. Nor did the fact that the mother very clearly disapproved. She brought him no rice that night. And he did not notice.

The next day, Leonid and the Scot awoke next to one another at roughly the same time. Everyone else was gone. They looked at each other conspiratorially. The Scotsman spoke first.

'Good shite, yeah?'

'Very good, yes.'

'Hey, I didnae catch yer name, pal. Mine's Johnny.'

'I am called Leonid.'

'Right. Like th' fellow with th' bushy brow, yeah?'

'Like Brezhnev, yes.'

'Well, Leo, it looks like it's time fer me to go t'work now.' With this, Johnny rose to leave.

'Wait!' Leonid looked up fearfully. 'Do not go. Not safe. And what about dragon ...'

'Aye. Another addict born.' Johnny smiled and looked around the space. 'Tell ye what, this is nae such a bad place t'crash. I'll be back this way before th' shelling starts in. Good?'

Leonid nodded, somewhat reassured.

'Hey, I'd also like to get me some shots of youse, together with yer family. Would youse mind?'

Leonid laughed. 'Of course not! Just bring dragon. Then I will let you to shoot me with gun.'

'Ha! Right, well, I'm aff, then. Later.' Johnny grabbed his bag and his cameras and scurried out the window.

Leonid leaned back and wondered whether or not his so-called family was ever coming back, and whether or not he even wanted them to.

❀

Later, when mother and daughter returned together, Leonid could read in their faces a sense of relief at finding Johnny gone. They had no idea he was now Leonid's new best friend.

The mother made a fire. She put some snow in the pot and melted it down. Then she poured out some water into the teacup, and took it to Leonid. He drank deep from it, and asked for more, which she dutifully brought him twice more before she and her daughter finally slaked their own thirst. Having done that, they started cooking the last of the rice.

The boy came back from his own hunt just as the modest dinner was nearly prepared. His mother looked at him; he shook his head. He had, evidently, been unable to obtain any nourishment. Leonid took this in, realizing it might mean that they were about to have their last meal for some time. As it was, they were all half-starved. The boy's failure could very well be the deathblow. They ate solemnly that night.

Leonid was unconcerned by all this. He was becoming agitated. The sun had fallen and the shelling had begun, but still there was no sign of his dealer. *He must have been killed, the fool! What am I doing to deserve this? Why must I always, always be paired with idiots? Pair me with a smart person for once!*

Johnny did not show, and Leonid passed another bad night, although not quite as intense as the others. He was nearly all the way back down, now – back to the sober life.

●

It was around seven o'clock in the morning when Johnny came back in through the basement window, awakening everyone but Leonid. The mother did not hide her displeasure at his reappearance. Before he could even bid them 'good morning', she began berating him in her own tongue, and loudly. This, from a woman who had barely whispered ten sentences in the previous few days! It was a frightening sight. She was loud enough to wake the dead. And wake they did.

Leonid jolted back to consciousness to find the startled, helpless Scot backed into a corner before the screaming woman. He got to his feet as quickly as he could.

'Leo, man, talk to th' missus for me, won't ye!'

'I told you already once, is not my wife.'

Leonid put his hand on the woman's shoulder, gently. She turned to look at him. Between them passed a silent moment as they shared a look usually reserved for husbands and wives. Through the eyes alone, she understood that Leonid needed Johnny's drugs to get him through. And again, through the eyes alone, he understood that she would accept this, but did not approve of it. She finally nodded and went to make the day's fire.

'Wha' ... feck was that? Ye didnae tell her our arrangement?'

Leonid ignored the question. He had his own. 'Why did you not come here last night?'

'Ah. Got myself trapped in someone's empty flat. Firefight. Got some good shots, though!' Johnny tapped his camera bodies together as he said this. 'Left early in the morn, after everyone was aff their heids with drink.'

'Did you bring dragon?'

'Why? Ye need some, do ye? Och, I'm only kidding wi' ye. Of course I've got it. Need tae pick up some more thamorra, though. I've a Chechen contact. Good, pure stuff. And cheap, too.'

This, at once, comforted Leonid, and got him thinking. 'Can you get vodka from contact?'

'No, that's strictly for themselves. What they dinnae drink, they sell or trade wi' th' Russkis at top dollar. More alcoholics than junkies in th' army, ye see.'

'I know this well,' Leonid replied despondently.

'Scag is healthier stuff, anyway.'

Now that he was done with his own questioning, done with his own needs, Leonid turned the subject over to the needs of the others in the room. 'Can you obtain any food? For them ...' He waved his good arm towards his new 'family'.

'Food is very scarce; only have what I brought into Grozny meself. Freeze-dried stuff, energy bars and th' like. Be happy tae share it oot, though.' With that, he opened his bag and showed Leonid what was on offer. It looked to be about three days' worth – for one person.

'I've no' really been eatin' all that much. Th' scag, ye know, it destroys yer appetite. I'd suggest the energy bars at this time of day. Breakfast o' champions.'

Leonid accepted three bars and presented them to the mother. She smiled broadly and bowed her head. This embarrassed him terribly, so he walked away from her. She and the children ate greedily; it was the first food with any actual taste or flavour to it that they'd consumed in over two weeks.

Across the room, Leonid watched anxiously as Johnny packed the aluminium.

○

Two days after Johnny's food rations had run out, the children began to cry from hunger. The mother went out on the hunt daily, but could find nothing. She tried to comfort them, hugged them to her breast, but their pangs were unendurable, and their wailing clearly soul-destroying. Leonid watched as she suffered a mother's greatest shame and fear: not being able to look after her own. That feeling completely dimmed her own hunger.

Johnny and Leonid hadn't had a bite in days themselves. They were doing quite well on their diet of water and heroin. They would have been doing a lot better were it not for the children's din. *It's worse than the fucking shelling!* In the end, Leonid struck upon a solution.

'Johnny … What if we gave them for to smoke? That would make them to stop with screaming? Would shut them up?'

'It would shut up King fecking Kong, aye! But they're only wee bairns …'

'They are starving children! Look on us. We do not require foods. That what works – works!'

Johnny could not argue with that calibre of logic, not in a war zone. He nodded and began making them a child-sized portion, or what he believed such a quantity would resemble, at any rate.

Leonid walked over to the mother. He knelt before her and slowly offered up the packed foil with great care, as gently as possible. Her gaze tore through him, and he froze under it. She slapped the foil from his hand violently, into the fire, and cursed him in her language. For the first time, he understood every word.

Johnny jumped in after it, and nearly burned his hands trying to get the junk back. The tar was already smoking; it was too late. Johnny grabbed his ten-pound note instead, and sucked as much of the opiate into his lungs as possible. The tenner, too close to the flames, quickly caught fire, and in mere seconds was no more. The dragon could not be chased.

'Feckin' hell!' Johnny wailed, and went back into the corner to pack a fresh hit. Surely he would need one now.

Leonid, still frozen to the spot, just stared at the mother. He was consumed with shame at having made the offer, and couldn't comprehend his own stupidity. *Of course she would react in this manner! How could I miss that? I must be high as a kite!* In Russian, he said repeatedly: 'I'm sorry. I'm so sorry!' But the mother had already turned away from him some time before. Her screaming was done. Leonid knew she would never again offer him help. He would never again win her over to his side.

Johnny announced that the hit was ready, and Leonid went over to join him.

The following day, as her children's pain deepened, the mother looked at the two junkies in amazement. How, she wondered, could they go this long without complaint, without food? With nothing but water, and that vile drug? What magic properties did it hold?

Her thoughts ran like that for most of the day. The idea of the heroin as a solution was slowly wearing down her resolve. This change in perspective was happening at such a slow rate that she herself didn't even realize it. She also didn't realize that she, who had consumed none of the drug, had gone hungry nearly as long as the junkies, with no complaint.

❁

On the fourth day of her children's torment, the mother could bear no more. She woke Leonid from his pleasant dreams and motioned for him to administer the drug to her babies. He did not argue. He knew it would cure their pain and ease their minds.

The mother watched nervously as her children inhaled deeply from the foil. Was she doing the right thing? Would this even work? Her thoughts raced, and her chest tightened. But almost at once, the children became silent, and she breathed freely again.

Then Leonid turned to her and held the foil under her chin. Declining, she pushed aside the pipe he offered. It was one thing for the children to drink from that well – they were innocents – but she would not be tainted by drugs, alcohol or any other depressant or stimulant. She would live through the day just as God had presented it to her. No more. No less.

❁

This scenario continued on, uninterrupted, for days. The mother would wake up and tend to Leonid's wound, kiss her sleeping children and then head out alone in a desperate search for nourishment. As each day passed, she now feared not only their starvation, but also that her children were becoming addicts. The kids never awoke with her anymore, but then, they never really slept. They were in a deep narcosis that essentially kept their lives on hold. Heroin had its finger on the pause button.

Johnny and Leonid would usually come out of their stupor at about the same time. Johnny would venture out to do his work; Leonid would just lie there, wreck that he was with his bound arm and beat-up face, and think things through in a half-stoned fashion.

He was still trying to piece together what had led him down this muddy, shit-covered track. Did Miki set him up? Despite all the evidence, Leonid could not or would not answer that question. He knew that the Mafiya had many arms, and at least one of them consisted of anti-Russian, militant Muslim Chechens: Borzoi's people. Leonid was not stupid, he could read the writing on the wall. Still, Miki had been a better father to him than his own. (Then again, it was not so difficult to beat out a man who, on several occasions, would refer to you as 'walking cum spillage'.) He couldn't fathom that Miki would not only set up those soldiers, but Leonid and Spaska too. After all, drunk as he had been, he remembered that those rooftop Chechens had taken very specific aim at his truck. As if they didn't want them to escape. As if they wanted no witnesses to the slaughter. As if someone had told them to ensure this.

Even so, he would not believe it.

He still had the card that Andrei Trofimov from America had given him. On a daily basis, he would pull it out of his shirt pocket and stare at the thing, dreaming of America while trying to forget Russia, forget Chechnya.

The mother returned empty-handed just as the children's sleep left them. Johnny was not far behind her, popping back in through the window at dusk. Then everyone, save the mother, got wasted again. Seven days. The routine had not changed in the slightest.

❁

On the eighth day, however, Johnny threw a monkey wrench into the tightly-run operation. He came in through the window and declared that the war was over. He explained that the Russians had dropped two massive bombs on the Chechen stronghold, the Presidential Palace. The back of the Chechen resistance was broken, and only a few small units remained in the city. They might still be able to hold out up in the mountains, but the battle for the city was clearly over and with it, Johnny's job.

(He didn't know how wrong his predictions would prove; the Chechens were a tough bunch, and the war would continue – even in Grozny – for two more years before Yeltsin would throw in the towel and sign a peace treaty. Then it would start up all over again a few years later, because wars never really end, they just move from place to place.)

Johnny announced his departure. He had his pics, he'd done his work and he was craving his London flat. Leonid begged and Leonid pleaded, but the Scotsman had his mind solidly made up. He was off and out of the shite. He entrusted to Leonid what little junk was left, bowed to the mother and the kids and was about to take leave – when something stopped him. Fucked up on the H, he'd forgotten to take shots of the ragtag family with whom he'd been living all this time. He also knew they were about to do their

81

thing, and it occurred to him what great and saleable shots those would be.

So he crouched down and shot the foursome, using a wide lens. The mother had her back to the scene as always, and Leonid was administering to the children. A soft, pleasant light came off the fire. He knew the photos would be hauntingly beautiful. Johnny was satisfied. He said farewell again, and stood to leave.

'You do not want hit before to leave?' asked Leonid.

'Nah, pal. Got to keep the oul' head on straight now. Rough terrain tae cross. Ta, all th' same! Cheers, all!'

With that, just as quickly as he had entered their lives and their cellared existence, Johnny was gone.

(What none of those he left behind would ever know was that those last photos were destined to show up in a famous German news magazine; but the caption would mention nothing of Chechnya, or of the war. Instead, it would read: 'Family life in the new Russia', and the accompanying article would claim the shots had been taken in Moscow. Something else Leonid would never know was that a certain beautiful woman with whom he had once been acquainted in Dresden would stumble upon that photo and exclaim: 'Was zum Teufel!')

✸

Leonid didn't really need the drugs anymore; his withdrawal from alcohol was long over and quite successful, and he was not yet addicted to the H. But now he, like the children, faced another foe: hunger. The three of them thus continued using, in an effort to assuage their fears regarding that enemy. The mother, as always, looked away helplessly.

✺

Strangely, she found food within twenty-four hours of Johnny's flight. The shortages had ended along with that particular phase of Chechen resistance; some of the black-marketers had found their way back into the city, and the marketplace was teeming once again.

In the face of this, the mother was unconcerned about whether or not the city was under the control of Chechens or Russians. She thought only of Johnny: within twenty-four hours of his arrival, there was no food to be had. Twenty-four hours after he'd gone, sustenance was theirs again. It was too much for it to be coincidence, she thought. With Johnny had come heroin and other troubles, and, to her way of thinking, this made him a devil of sorts. An evil spirit. Call it superstition, but that's how it worked out in her mind. And she, in succumbing to his wiles by letting herself be tempted by him, even if only for the sake of her babies, had committed a great sin, an unforgivable one. She should have been stronger, shown more courage, more faith. This is what she told herself.

When she returned, the children were just coming out of their netherworld. Leonid was about to start packing up the aluminium. She showed everyone the food she'd purchased and ordered her daughter to commence with its preparation, which the girl did, groggily. The mother then stamped over to Leonid, held out an open palm and stared deeply into his eyes. It was, as usual, their only means of communication, and he understood immediately. He knew it would be impossible not to give her what she was after, and handed it over.

She took the small bundle and climbed out through the window. All three of those left in the cellar looked at each other guiltily. At once, with their eyes, they formed a pact that would not be broken. Everything, forthwith, must be done in deference to the mother. As the daughter continued stoking the fire, the boy got to his feet and went to collect snow for the pot. Even Leonid got up, looked around and, having found no useful chore to carry out individually, helped the daughter with the fire.

That night, as on the difficult nights that had come before, they ate in silence – except the mother, who did not eat at all. She was punishing herself for her transgression, the Johnny transgression. Yet everyone else in the room interpreted her actions otherwise. They felt her abstinence was their own punishment, her way of admonishing them for their own transgressions. They willingly accepted the reproach.

In the end, then, everyone was only really punishing themselves. How truly like a family they were, now more than ever, all misunderstanding one another, each bearing the weight of the entire group. Well, perhaps less so Leonid: He was still trying to figure out where the mother had jettisoned his stash.

❁

Over the following weeks, the basement dwellers noticed a gradual swing of Russian artillery in their direction. The explosions were becoming more pronounced every day. Occasionally, when they ventured outside, they would see a plume of smoke above the neighbouring rooftops.

The mother and children spoke amongst themselves about the idea of seeking out new shelter. The kids had been prematurely made adults by war, so their mother did not think twice about consulting them and weighing their opinions. She had noticed the change in them long ago.

As they discussed the issue with greater animation than Leonid had observed in them previously, he couldn't help wondering what was afoot. They weren't leaving Leonid out in the cold, so to speak – it was just the usual problem of language. In any case, the prospects of finding new and adequate shelter in Grozny were so grim that they were unable to come to a decision.

The Russians helped them conquer their indecisiveness a few days later, when a shell hit a building four doors down. That was it. They would migrate to the neighbouring republic of Ingushetia, to the west. Enough with Grozny! They would take Leonid with them, despite the fact that his arm still needed some more time in its improvised splint, and that he might slow them down, putting them in further danger. The mother would find whatever food and extra clothing she could within the next twenty-four hours, and then they would leave. Everyone agreed; everyone but Leonid, who remained in the dark.

❂

Leonid watched them closely the following day. All the preparations they were making, all the hustle and bustle: he couldn't figure it out. His cluelessness was beginning to cause him no small amount of anxiety – so much so that he was in complete disbelief when, an hour before dusk, which is when the shelling would normally begin, they got him to his feet and led him towards the window. *She's still angry about the dragon-chasing!* He imagined they were excommunicating him, offering him up as a human sacrifice. As they cajoled him he resisted – but they understood his actions as little as he did theirs. The family looked each to the other, baffled, but they persisted, and after much effort they managed to coax him up through the window and pushed him outside.

Even then, he pleaded: 'No! No! You can't do this!'

Leonid was behaving way over the top, as he always did when he wasn't apathetic – which was usually, but only when it was not his own ass on the line. This was not such a time.

'I was only trying to help! Johnny – it was Johnny's drugs! It's his fault, not mine! You can't punish the innocent like this, you can't push me under a bomb!'

He lay in the snow, weeping and refusing to get up. They struggled to lift him with great difficulty, then attempted to help him down the street. There was no time for such theatrics; the shelling would soon recommence, and they needed to get ahead of it.

Leonid began to panic, such that he could not see that they were leaving *with* him, abandoning the basement all together. He pictured them delivering him to their contacts, their Chechen overlords. He kept arguing with them and begging them, but as much as they tried to calm his fears, they could not get through to him, either with smiling faces or soothing tones and gentle words. They were making little progress, and now dusk was upon them.

Leonid broke free from them and ran back towards the cellar. The boy chased him. A shell shuddered on the ground behind Leonid, knocking him ass over tits.

When the dust began to clear, he found himself suddenly less panicked, and he looked back. The boy was on the ground, gasping and convulsing, his lower body rendered into nothingness. Within moments, it was over. He bled out, and another shell screamed in the air somewhere above him.

Leonid could not see the mother or daughter through the haze and distance. He imagined he could make out their vague forms down the street, but just as they were coming into sharper focus, a new shell hit the side of a building between them and enshrouded them anew.

He heard more shells incoming and began to move quickly in the other direction, away from the mother and daughter. He didn't ever want to face them again, but still, he kept looking over his shoulder, wondering if they knew about the boy.

A few more explosions, and the street was no more. Now Leonid was running. Alone.

Six

Leonid ran blindly all through the night, between the dark city streets. Every so often a shell would explode ahead of him or to either side, forcing him to alter his course. He tried to move as far away as possible from the violence but it was always there, at every corner. He was like a lab rat coursing through a labyrinth, electric shocks imminent at every bad turn.

He ran and ran, hoping to come upon some sensible Russian soldiers who could help him out of his predicament, maybe even help him get back to Moscow. The problem was, never having been too clever with directions, he'd become so turned around during the bombardment that he had inadvertently put himself behind the Chechen line.

He only realized this early in the morning, after throwing himself upon the mercy of a fighter he had mistaken for Russian. This was not as foolish as it seemed: Russian and Chechen soldiers wore the same winter fatigues. They had, after all, once served under the same banner. The only things that might differentiate them in appearance were the jihadist bandanas that some Chechens now tied around their heads and helmets. There was the small matter of language, too. It was this difference that tipped off Leonid to his mistake;

when, too late, he remarked on the bandana as well, he lost all hope. Surely he would die.

The Chechen fighter, however, could not be bothered: he had other Russians on his mind. He had thrown Leonid off, pushing him in the direction of inner Chechnya along with a downtrodden mass of refugees from the land. He never even noticed that Leonid was ethnic Russian and hence a possible spy.

Leonid continued onward, towards a forest in the distance. To the best of his ability, he tried to hold those bearings for the many days and weeks to follow. He told himself he'd walk a straight line until he came out of Chechnya.

But no one ever walks a straight line in a forest.

✿

Leonid was now far from Grozny the terrible, out in the countryside. Although the shelling was now fainter and the heavy fighting further away, he did not feel any more secure. He was a city boy, and felt right only with pavement beneath his feet. Of country life – the ways of woodsmen, of pig and potato farmers – he knew nothing. In fact, he often mocked them, as city folk tend to do. As a student under the Soviets, he and his comrades read Tolstoy and – secretly – referred to him as a 'rich fucking nutter' for working in the fields alongside the peasants. Here was Leonid now, wandering through an endless wood, wishing he had a clue.

That memory came back to him, still not fully realized, of walking with his grandfather. As he put one foot in front of the other, he dwelled on it, earnestly trying to remember what his grandfather had tried to impress upon him that day, what he was trying to *impart*. Although he still could not touch upon the thing, it comforted him somewhat.

Morning. He had marched through the night yet again, the adrenaline in his bloodstream ensuring that he felt no fatigue. But now he was slowing down, allowing himself some time to think. Where would he sleep tonight? He realized he was quite cold. How to make a fire? He felt his stomach rumbling. What could he eat out here? This was the same variety of questions he had found himself asking upon realizing he was stranded in Grozny, questions of vital importance that most people never needed to ask, which arise as a result of war or extreme poverty. All of them needed answering once again. Back in Grozny, he had felt as though his life had been reduced to zero, that he had been forced to learn to live differently. But this was not Grozny. These woods had effectively re-zeroed him.

It's an curious thing the way a person, a brain, a mind, will begin to observe and problem-solve when faced with desperation. Ask anyone who has survived some ghastliness what saved them; when you hear their replies, you will undoubtedly ask, in amazement: 'How in bloody hell did you ever think of that!?' The answer is always the same: because they had to.

So it was with Leonid. Never having thought of arboreal things for even a single moment in his life, he now observed the shape and angling of the taller conifers' branches that towered above him, and took an interest in the smaller conifers, the lower branches of which actually swept the ground. It occurred to him that there must be a tent-like space between the trunks of these smaller trees and those branches. He got down by the nearest tree, bent some of its lower branches upwards – one arm clumsy in the deteriorating splint – and crawled inside. He was pleased to find that there was indeed space to lie down there, and that on top of that, the ground was dry and still covered with scrubby grass rather than snow. He found, as well, that the pine needle-laden branches cut the wind significantly when latticed densely over one another. Quite proud of himself at having solved the shelter question for the coming night, and recognizing it as a convenient hiding place should any bad business arise, he lay down to rest.

His nap turned into a sort of hibernation from which he did not stir until evening, finally awoken by a mild shivering. He left his shelter to think, rubbing his arms and pacing about for warmth. Although the frost blowing off the mountains could not reach him, there was still the matter of winter temperatures. He needed a fire, but how to build one without leaving the shelter? City boy he might have been, but he still had, at least, some basic common sense. Any fire built under a dry pine would surely turn into an inferno. Should he therefore move into an open space and build his fire, or remain where he was? He deliberated the matter for the better part of an hour before the answer came to him.

He began by determining the direction of the wind, then set about snapping off branches on the leeward side of his tree, which offered him no protection from the gusts. He broke them off all the way up to his own height and bashed the snow from the branches higher up with a long stick. Digging a small pit under the now-bald side of the tree, he layered its base with evenly spaced rocks to keep water away from the flames. He then built a pyramid, in the centre of soft, dry pine needles from the tree's base.

With the matches left to him by the thieves who had taken his cigarettes that first night in Grozny, Leonid started his first-ever fire. He began with a little spark of the pine-needle tinder, then slowly added sections of twigs and thicker branches he found lying on the ground nearby. He kept the fire small, just enough to warm himself, so that it wouldn't set the branches ablaze above him. Piling a few of the thicker pieces of wood around the edges of the pit to dry out in preparation for later, he sat back to admire his handiwork.

Briefly, as he watched the flames dance, he wondered how he had managed to concoct all this, and whether or not, perhaps, this was the thing his grandfather had taught him. Yet upon further reflection, he realized that his grandfather had been much like him – a creature of the city. *Grandfather would never have thought of this. No. This was my idea.* Leonid lay back and basked in the warmth. It was starting to get dark. What with all the work and thought he'd put into his new home, he drifted off in minutes, and in sleep he appeared almost – dare we say it – content.

How is it that human ingenuity, the reason that chops away at our pure animal tendencies, the curiosity that promotes creative, inventive and beneficial thinking, is *always* put into action only of necessity? Only when a man is put into critical circumstances does the brain kick in. *Always*, it is only when he must save himself that something pops out of his mind that advances him, or humanity, towards the greater good. When the very same man is in comfortable repose, none of this mental activity takes place: *never* a thought for others who might be in harm's way, *never* that crucial synthesizing idea that everything in the world is connected to everything else, *never* the understanding that if one suffers, we all lose a share of our own spirit. *Never* do we understand this, until we ourselves are the ones doing the suffering. *Never* the shelter or the fire, unless we have serious need of them.

Unless Leonid had need of them.

Always the blind eye to those in need, to whom we feel no obligation.

Perhaps we should soften that a bit. Terms such as *always* and *never* are a bit excessive in their absolute qualities. Let us forgo hyperbole and exchange them for a more just word, though not much happier a truth: that word is *usually*.

❁

Leonid found his new dwelling quite acceptable, and, having put so much thought and effort into creating it, he decided to stay for a while – at least until his arm had completely healed. Of course, one problem still remained unsolved. *Always one more thing.* There was the matter of food. He'd managed to ignore his hunger, but now he was ravenous.

He wondered how many more times he'd have to face these questions. Shelter, clothing, food. The same shitty cycle, over and over. It was becoming a full-time job, and Leonid felt it would soon break him. *When will all these fucking considerations stop!*

The answer, of course, was *never*. We all live this way, never seeing it for what it is until something happens to turn our world on its head. There might well be other things, some might say more important things, such as friendship, compassion, sex, even love. But best to save all that nonsense for when and if you survive the ordeal and come out on the other side. Get yourself nice and cosy in front of a television, and then you can worry about where your next blowjob is coming from and whether or not you should throw a dinner party the following weekend.

On his third day of deprivation, Leonid pondered the fact that, although snow covered the ground elsewhere, he still had green grass under his tree. He realized slowly that all the other trees of this genus must conceal similar offerings. After wondering about cows, goats, sheep and all the other animals that ate the stuff, he asked himself if it could really be so bad. Like an animal, then, he began to eat it. Still not sated when he had finished mowing his own lawn, he moved on to the next tree and chewed around the trunk of that one.

He spent all night shitting green liquid, and in the morning was forced to reassess his diet.

That's when he discovered pine cones. At first, Leonid had to smash them against stones to get at the nuts inside. Then he learned, quite accidentally, by leaving a pile of cones by the fire, that they opened naturally when warm. Bland they might have tasted to him, but at least they seemed nutritious. He also found a fresh stream nearby, which provided the best water he'd ever tasted. No more sucking on snowballs for him.

Along the banks of the stream he noticed a dense stand of cattails, and remembered their nickname: 'Cossack asparagus'. He tried eating one, digging the root out of the muddy water and peeling into the white core. The taste wasn't exactly pleasant, but it was definitely edible. He grabbed a bunch and returned to the shelter.

Although he had actually become quite comfortable – as comfortable as one can be under such conditions – over the weeks his arm had healed. He knew it was time to start thinking about venturing out into the world again.

During his time in the forest, he had barely been able to make out the sounds of war, and he sometimes wondered whether or not the whole bloody affair had blown over. Maybe life was back to normal and here he was, sitting under a fucking pine tree like some kind of Slavic Robinson Crusoe. But then a low-flying gunship would pass overhead, and his imaginings would evaporate.

Another big difference between his current situation and the one in Grozny was that, back there, fear had been a constant. It was breathed into him at every waking moment, and even invaded his dreams. Now he knew only boredom. When you have nothing to do all the day long but people are trying to kill you, well, that just sucks the tedium right out of it. Fear is all that's really needed to preoccupy the mind. Take away the murderers and the bombs, and what you have left is a big, empty black hole to send your mind reeling. And much of the time, he filled that hole with thoughts of Miki.

When he was sure his ulna was in one piece again, he lost no time in bidding *adieu* to his self-made home and the damn pine cones. As he looked upon it for the very last time in the early morning light with pride, a thought occurred to him: he wished he had a camera. The boys back home would not believe how he had made do in the Caucasus. He could scarcely believe it himself.

Turning his back on his accomplishment, he set himself in what he deemed to be a westerly direction. He wanted

Ingushetia and was quite sure he was facing it, so off he marched – into what was, in fact, a southerly direction, into the mountains

As noted previously, Leonid was lousy at directions.

❂

The Chechen soldier stared at him scornfully as he dialled the phone. Leonid sat before this man, bleeding from his nose and, once again, his forehead. They had reopened the almost-healed scab from the truck collision. Two other soldiers had their weapons trained on him. The phone call would determine Leonid's fate.

What are these assholes doing this far west, anyway? I was sure the Russians held this area. Fuck! My bad luck never ends!

Earlier that morning, Leonid had finally left the forest and come upon a paved road, which he decided to follow what he thought was north. He had figured this would surely put him, if not in Ingushetia, then certainly into contact with the Russian army. The road, however, had other plans. Because the road, of course, ran east–west.

After about an hour, he came upon a quiet roadside shack. Its door was slightly ajar, and it appeared to be empty. Having now walked for over seventeen hours with little rest, he thought it an excellent place to crash.

Upon entering, however, he found three Chechen men lying in various parts of the room, passed out. Empty vodka bottles were strewn about the floor. He wondered for a brief moment whether or not these were from his truck, but this thought was quickly pushed aside by more urgent concerns. His entrance into the shack had provoked no stirring, so he slowly began to back out.

That was when his eye, always quick in these matters, caught an unopened bottle of vodka lying on its side atop a table. He stopped dead. He could already taste it. *This is madness.* But the alcoholized part of his brain chimed in with all manner of cheap justifications. *If that bottle should roll off and break on the floor, it would certainly wake them. That fucking bottle could get someone caught!* Too true.

He inched up to the table extremely slowly. Reaching it, he picked up the bottle carefully, making sure not to let it thud against the tabletop in any way. He then turned around and went back towards the door, checking on the sleeping men. What he should have been checking was the floor below him; his foot hit the topside of an empty, throwing him off balance and sending his ass to the floor with a loud thump. That thump, combined with the thunderous sound of the empty rolling on the wooden floorboards, was still not enough to wake the piss-headed soldiers.

That was where his luck failed once again: his tripping-up had sent the precious vodka bottle flying. Now he could only watch in horror as it broke its holding pattern and came down in slow motion for a smooth crash-landing. Leo grimaced against the sound of the shattering glass, which woke the soldiers.

After administering the requisite beating, the soldiers called their superiors in the hopes that they would be instructed to execute the idiot who had done in their last remaining bottle. To their frustration, they were told to keep him on ice until further notice. Angered by this dispatch, they agreed uniformly to give him yet another beating; this one was on the house.

✿

The prisoner is to be moved to such-and-such a place. He will be kept there for further interrogation. There have been reports of spies in the region. He is not to be touched. He will be picked up shortly.

These were, in brief, the orders that had come down from on high. Unfortunately, by the time they'd arrived, the soldiers were well into their third round on Leonid. Now they'd have to clean him up and make him all pretty for their superiors.

He waited there with them for the better part of a week. Their moods lightened and their lust for his blood abated when they had another case of vodka delivered, but Leonid became quite vexed as he was unable to get his hands on any of it.

He could not suppress the idea that the vodka was his, that it had come from his truck. *Nostrovya, you fucking murderous shits. Go ahead, get drunk, pass out. You'll see what happens.* These were, of course, foolish thoughts. Leonid was hogtied, lying on his side on the floor.

Sometimes they gave him a little water and maybe a bite or two of bread, but that was all. He lay there on the floorboards, enviously watching as they drank themselves into a stupor day after day: all he'd ever really wanted for himself in the world.

His death sentence once again stayed but not commuted, Leonid grew somewhat confident. As each day passed, he knew he would live to see another. So what if it should turn out worse than the previous one? So fucking what! He'd spent too much time these last few months obsessing over his own death and living in fear. He was glad that the

Chechens had nabbed him and beaten his bloody brains out. He was gladder still that he had reached out to grab from the gods that which was rightfully his, the vodka bottle.

He would indeed come out the other side of this, though he had no idea where that was. His fear had left him. He breathed it all in and blew it all out. Or thought he had, anyway.

SEVEN

The truck sped along a muddy track into a dense forest. Leonid bounced up and down in the back, banging his already aching cranium against the non-upholstered metal ceiling. The only thing cushioning the repeated blows to any effect was the potato sack he wore over his head. His captors' precautions were pointless, as Leonid was already lost beyond recovery, not to mention redemption.

He felt the vehicle stop. The soldiers pulled him out roughly, marched him into a building of some kind and plopped him down in a chair. Only then was the sack removed. He found himself seated in front of a weasley-looking bureaucrat, and, unexpectedly, this gave him some measure of hope.

'Name?' This, in accented Russian.

'Leonid.'

'Full name!'

'Leonid Petrovich Koshkin.' In answering truthfully, he surprised himself.

'You are KGB.' It was not a question but an assertion, to be confirmed or denied. Unsure as to which response would be preferable, Leonid decided to remain on the periphery.

'There is no more KGB. You must mean the FSB.'

'Yes, yes. You are that, then!'

He thought it over for a few seconds. An eternity to the bureaucrat, Leonid could plainly see. 'No. No, I am not.'

'Are you mocking me?'

Leonid looked behind his chair and gave the two gun-toting Chechen guards in the room the once-over. They appeared to be more bored than anything else. 'I can only assume from your tone that it is your greatest wish, to be mocked.'

'Are you aware that you are facing execution for crimes against the Free Chechen State?'

'What!' Leonid had a lump in his throat now. He could only surmise that all this was about the attempted vodka theft. 'I have connections ... I'll repay the vodka tenfold! What is this!'

'We are not interested in your alcohol. We are Muslims. And you are an agent of the FSB, sent from Moscow!'

'I'm not from Moscow, nor am I a spy! I was born and raised right here in Grozny,' Leo lied. 'My whole fucking life is here!'

'We are not in Grozny. Have you forgotten? There is no Grozny. Not anymore.'

'This is fucking nonsense! I demand to be released to my unit in Grozny! Immediately!'

'And which unit would that be, comrade?'

Leonid just looked at his interrogator dumbly. The bureaucrat sighed and made a signal to the guards. Then the lights went out.

He awoke in an unfamiliar room. Slowly, through his grogginess, he became aware of two other human forms.

They were both high above him, tending to his wounds. He was sure they were vivisecting him, and, always the screamer, Leonid began emitting horrible sounds as though he actually was being tortured.

The figures backed away from him, speaking to him in gentle tones until he calmed down a bit. He checked his torso for open holes, missing limbs and whatever other terrible disfiguration his imagination could conjure up. As his sight came back into focus, he saw the man and woman clearly.

The woman asked him in flawless Russian if he was all right. He eyed her suspiciously; after several moments of hesitation, he replied that he was.

The man then spoke to her in American-accented English, enquiring whether or not Leonid had been tortured. She began, but was cut short by Leonid's laughter. Always paranoid, he was certain this was a Chechen trick. He glared at the pair and said, in Russian: 'Yes, yes! I speak English! I understand everything that goes on here. Everything! This charade is not necessary, and it proves nothing! Yes, I know English. But that alone does not make a spy of me!'

The man and the woman exchanged knowing glances, and seemed to agree silently that this one had really been worked over and was surely delusional.

'He's a bit banged up. He doesn't know where he is. Let him settle in a bit. We'll talk with him later.' The woman said this to the man in English, as though Leonid wasn't there.

'Hey! You there! Cocksucker! Don't condescend to me, bitch! I know exactly where I am. I can promise you that your tricks won't work on me! I know how you Chechens operate. How? Because I was born here! I learned English. I am no fucking spy!'

'But no one is accusing you of –' the woman began.

'And they had better not!' Leonid interrupted her. 'I'm as Chechen as anyone in this fucking room!'

She snickered despite herself, but Leonid was unfazed. He ranted on sporadically in this vein for the next few hours. The American stopped paying him any attention, but his translator seemed to find some amusement in Leonid's outbursts. Entertainment of any sort will fit the bill when you're facing the unknown.

✹

Leonid's paranoia ebbed after some time, when he finally began to notice the others' appearances. Their bruises, and their bloodied and ragged clothing, eventually wore down his belief that they could be grouped in with his tormentors. Yes, he was now certain: these were fellow prisoners, people like him.

Slowly, he drew them into conversation. He asked the banal sorts of questions that strangers on a train might exchange. When they were satisfied that he had calmed down, they kept up their own part of the Q & A. In this way, Leonid learned how they were situated in normal life, and of their current predicament. And, in this way, they learned virtually nothing of Leonid's own story. Nothing true anyway.

Eva, as the woman was called, acted as a translator for the American, whose name was Bill Hanson. Eva was of Georgian descent, and of very little interest to Leonid. However, the American fired his curiosity. As Eva prattled on about this and that, and the civil war in Georgia, he nodded absently, staring at the man – whose sense of chivalry made him insist that she speak first. Leonid was beside himself, lusting for Hanson's words of America.

Finally, Hanson's turn came. Although Eva, who appeared to defer to Hanson, had spoken mostly of her role in helping him in his 'mission', as she had called it, he merely repeated her words. Still, it was all fresh and new to Leonid. Hanson was a relief worker of great experience and even notoriety. He was here to help the people of Grozny, Leonid was told, and, if possible, to contain the war, to stop it from spreading throughout Chechnya.

Leonid laughed inwardly. *As if there could ever be any relief of Chechnya!* But although he found the man's idealism somewhat foolish, he still respected him. Why? Because he was an American. Because he was the thing that Leonid wished to be.

When Leonid truthfully (and finally) revealed himself as a Muscovite, Hanson grew excited. He bombarded him with a flurry of rather detailed questions about life in Russia. What was his opinion on the availability of meat? Of the prices? Was public transport running better or worse than in the former USSR? How difficult was it to buy a new flat? What was the availability of household appliances like? And what of the non-faulty appliances?

And so on, and so forth. Leonid found this barrage all very strange. At first he assumed the man was keen on moving to Moscow, but then some of his questions struck him as rather personal (particularly the one about faulty appliances). He became reticent, then stopped answering altogether. This did not hinder Hanson. He kept the questions coming fast and hard. It didn't even seem that he needed the answers; it seemed like he already had them.

Leonid's unease began to surge again. *Shit! This guy knows something. He's onto me.* He could not, however, have been further off the mark. Hanson, he could not have known, employed this routine with everyone he came into contact with, regardless of their station in life. He was a collector of the hard facts on all aspects of social welfare in every country he visited, and many he had not. His curiosity was inexhaustible. If there were problems, he would find solutions. He prided himself on being a fixer. It was his calling.

Although currently tackling the problem of Chechnya, and specifically the problem of evacuating the civilian population from Grozny, he still had many ideas for Russia, too, which he considered a powder keg, despite the Western politicians and press describing what was happening as a 'democratic renaissance'. He expounded widely upon the reasons for this, telling Leonid that huge mistakes had been made in the transition from communism to what it was today: not a democracy but a kleptocracy. Leonid knew a thing or two on that score. These mistakes, Hanson the American continued, went back well before the Berlin Wall came down, as far back as the early 1980s, if not earlier.

Leonid had come of age during that period, and remembered it well. He had to agree with all that Hanson said, and was amazed by his insight. He had no idea that such people existed in America. The realization only helped strengthen his desire to live there. *How unlike us these people are! They see a problem – they fix it! Us, we drink and complain and fall deeper into the shit.*

Hanson held court well into the night, speaking on a variety of subjects. About earthquakes in Mexico that devastated whole communities. About civil war in Angola. About infant mortality rates in India. For every one of these issues, and many others as well, he had solutions. Eva observed him admiringly, just as she had countless times over the past few months. She watched Leonid, too. Hanson had the gift of oratory; he commanded his audiences. Eva could see that Leonid was already a new convert.

And he was. He listened intently for hours about things he normally couldn't have been bothered with, because, after all, what did they have to do with him or his own problems? Yet, although he was not aware of it, the longer Hanson spoke, the more Leonid was slowly awakening, one degree at a time.

Leonid stirred, and found himself alone in the room with Eva. Although she had barely spoken the previous night, and despite the fact that all his attention had been focused on Hanson, Leonid had still managed to form an opinion of the woman: she had a cold and cynical manner, he'd decided. She was somehow judging him against the same high standard to which she held Hanson. In short, he felt she did not like him very much. He was not wrong.

'Sleeping Beauty awakes!'

Leonid chose to ignore this. 'Where's Hanson?'

'She looks about the castle, but Prince Charming is nowhere to be found.'

'Cut that shit out!' he shouted back.

Eva did not flinch. 'He's in there.' She pointed towards the door. 'For his daily interrogation. I've already had mine. You'll most likely be next.' She finished in English instead of their common tongue.

Leonid suddenly noticed her bloodied nose and shirtfront. He switched to English: 'Every day they are doing this?'

'It's been going on for five days now.'

'But for why?'

'They're convinced that we are Russian spies,' she said limply.

'But Hanson is *Amerikanski!*'

Eva shrugged. 'These Chechens are worse than Georgians. They see KGB everywhere.'

'Is anyone knowing that you are here?'

'They know that we're in Chechnya, yes. They know that we were expected back in Ingushetia three days ago, yes. Do they know that we're in a shack by the side of a dirt road? No.'

This made Leonid reappraise his own situation. No one knew where he was, no one was expecting him anywhere at anytime and no one gave a good goddamned shit. 'Shit,' he muttered.

'It could be worse ...'

'*Blyat!* Could it!'

With this, the door was flung open and Hanson was thrown back in. He collapsed on top of Leonid, clutching at his stomach. Eva rushed over and immediately began tending to him, whispering softly in his ear.

'Shall we have a word with the new guy?' asked the guard at the threshold, in Russian.

An unseen voice answered coldly from the other room: 'Leave him until tomorrow. He'll speak more freely after he sees how we deal with the other two.' Leonid shivered.

The guard smiled down at them all, and replied: 'Dostoevsky. Yes. He'll sing.' With that, he slammed the door shut, leaving the captives to wonder what this 'Dostoevsky' business might mean.

'It can't be good.' This was Eva's assessment.

Hanson straightened himself up and paced the room, trying to regain his wind. 'Thank God he didn't say "Kafka". Don't think I could hold out against any treatment of that sort.'

Eva gave a nervous laugh, and Hanson smiled weakly back at her. All these literary allusions were lost on Leonid, though of course he had read his Dostoevsky. *What the fuck is a 'kafka'?* Still, he was somewhat comforted by his companions' attempts at levity, even though it made him feel as if they were alone together in the room and that he was merely an invisible witness.

'Don't worry. They'll be coming for us any day now. Any day, Eva. Our friends are sure to find us.' Hanson continued to reassure her. She nodded, clearly unsure that this was anything but a brave face for her benefit. Leonid, excluded from the comforting words, took them to heart all the same. He figured Hanson to be his only good chance of escaping this mess, and a damn good one at that. He decided that whatever happened, no matter the circumstances, he would cleave himself to the other two. No matter what.

The three prisoners were roughly awakened at daybreak by several Chechen guards who barged into the room and forced them to their feet at gunpoint. They barely came to their senses as they were pushed outside and into the woods.

Two of the soldiers tied Leonid to a tree while a third held a pistol under his chin. Hanson and Eva were handed spades and ordered to dig two separate plots in a clearing. To the three captives, all this was happening as if in a dream. Time was at once shortened and lengthened, and before any of them were sure what had actually transpired, it was all over and the ditches were dug.

The commander stood across from them, at the head of the pits. Whereas the others in the group were unkempt and rowdy, the commander was clean-shaven and very composed; even as the youngest of them, he seemed the wisest. This is what scared Leonid most.

Kalashnikov rifles were poked into Hanson's and Eva's backs; they were made to kneel down before what was now clearly to be their respective eternal resting places.

'You will now admit to me that you are working in cooperation with Russian intelligence agencies.' The commander's voice was loud, but calm. Unnervingly calm. Leonid recognized it – the voice from the night before, the speaker who had gone unseen. With the cold gunmetal on his skin, the execution scene playing itself out before him and that voice – an affront to all humanity – in his ears, Leonid began to gag, attempting to hold back the bile that fear doles out. The commander continued: 'This is the last chance I am able to offer you. Tell him.'

Eva, trembling, haltingly translated the commander's words for Hanson. She needn't have bothered; he'd heard similar lines so many times that it had all just become old hat to him. Having fulfilled her duty to Hanson, she reverted back to Russian and begged for her life and for his, and vehemently and repeatedly denied the accusation.

Hanson had his eyes shut tight. He was chanting his usual mantra: 'Don't be scared, Eva.' He always made sure to speak her name, to pronounce it clearly. 'They won't harm us, Eva. Very shortly we will be released. Don't be afraid, Eva. Soon this will all be over.'

The commander repeated the accusation and added the obvious: 'Confess now or you will be shot.'

Leonid lost control of his throat and hoarked up a mouthful onto the hand that held the gun below his chin. The soldier reacted not with revulsion, but rather by sticking the gun directly into Leonid's mouth, shouting at him to watch the carnage, all without even wiping his hand clean.

For the third time, the commander put forth the accusation. Hanson broke off his mantra. His eyes still closed, he shouted his reply: 'We are here to help the Chechen civilian population, which is being devastated by this senseless fucking war! We have no connection to any intelligence agencies anywhere! We're here to help the Chechen people! We've done this before in other places, as I have told you! Check your records! Call your people! Do what you have to do! Just get your damn facts straight!'

'But we have done all that,' replied the commander in English, 'and the official story is that you are CIA. That you are here to find out about nuclear weapons, and that you do this in conjunction with the Russian government.'

Opening his eyes now and glaring at the commander, Hanson muttered in disgust: 'That is absolute bullshit.'

The commander gave a hint of a smile before turning his back. 'Do it,' he said.

Guns were cocked. Leonid's face was held so that he was forced to watch the scene. Eva began praying and Hanson resumed his mantra, trying to calm her. Shots were fired, and echoed through the woods. And soon, very soon after that, began the laughter. The soldiers were all laughing. The commander was not.

Eva broke down, weeping into the wet ground. Hanson crawled over shakily and embraced her. The commander began his speech: 'This was the punishment Fyodor Dostoevsky suffered at the hands of the Tsar. He was lucky. For him, he was only tricked once. Most other people were put in front of a firing squad and told they were going to die again and again, for days. Most never required shooting: they went mad within a week. Tomorrow, all that transpired today shall be repeated exactly the same way. The only things that may change are that I will have your confession, and that you may or may not be shot. These changes depend on you alone. Perhaps tomorrow you'll feel differently.' With this, the commander dismissed Hanson and Eva and walked over to Leonid. 'And you? If you don't start talking soon, what happens to them will happen to you. Only one day later. Think hard on that.'

Hanson and Eva were pushed back through the woods, towards the house. Both were shaking uncontrollably as they passed Leonid, still tied to the tree. They had not heard the commander's last words to him.

Leonid was surprised by the look of utter relief that washed over the faces of both both Hanson and Eva when he was eventually returned to the room. Hanson got up off the floor and gave him a bear hug, while Eva's eyes were glossy with tears.

Hanson said: 'Thank God you're still with us, son!'

Leonid was too tired to comprehend what they were on about. Filling the two graves had been nearly as hard as digging one, he reckoned.

'Sit down, son. Sit down.' Hanson ushered him into his usual corner and handed him a drink from the single water jug that the Chechens had allotted them. 'We've been expecting to hear a gunshot for the last two hours. When we didn't hear one, our thoughts grew morbid. There are hundreds of ways to kill a man, and almost all are worse than a bullet.'

'What in fuck you are talking on?' The water revived Leonid a bit.

'We thought they murdered you, you fool!' Eva shouted – a far cry from the quiet tears of a few minutes earlier.

'They did. With work. They made for me to fill the holes you dig.'

'They did *what?*'

'He told you, was not making joke. Everything the same tomorrow.'

Eva punched a wall and swore in Russian: 'Sons of bitches!'

Hanson slumped to the ground.

All of them understood now that they really would be made to play out this sick game over and over, and that it could only end in one fashion. Silence fell over the room as each considered that ending.

Leonid suddenly felt a sense of being equal to the others as he slowly recognized the look that had come over them when he returned unharmed. If he was OK, then they were OK. Just as he had earlier decided that his safety lay with them, they were clearly thinking the same thing about him. This idea pleased and comforted him.

Eva shook with fear and anger She had mentioned a daughter back in Georgia, and was thinking of her and the likelihood that the girl would become an orphan soon enough. She continued, sporadically, to punch the wall every time the pain in her breast overwhelmed her. Soon her knuckles were bleeding.

Hanson, refusing to think about tomorrow and exhausted from consoling Eva as he had done for nearly a week, needed a break. He looked to Leonid. 'What about you, Leonid?' he asked. 'What's your story?'

Leonid had spent the previous two days spellbound by Hanson's philosophy, political analysis and tales. Now, to be asked by the big man to speak of himself was really just too much: an honour that filled him with a sense of pride. He began, though reluctantly. He feared reproach – mostly from Eva's direction – but tried to stick to the facts. 'I was truck driver before the Wall coming down. Before all shit come down.'

'Go on. Were you married? Where did you live?'

'No, I never have wife.' He coughed and shifted his eyes up and to the right. Here, he lied. 'None of the girlfriends could be living with the idea. All knew of each other. They are not trusting in me.'

Eva was not listening, still in her own personal hell. Hanson chuckled, though. Already Leonid's bullshit was easing him out from under the weight of their ordeal. 'So you lived alone, then? In Moscow?'

'Not alone. In Moscow, I live with crippled father. The big war hero!'

'Afghanistan?'

'Of course, yes.'

'Mark you, we're going to see more trouble there.' Hanson had ideas about that country, too. 'And your mother? What of her?'

'Oh, he kill her, the hero. Put head through television glass.' Leonid lied about this nonchalantly.

'My God! I'm so sor –'

'He is probably dead too, in front television now.'

'Why is that?'

'Or dead in bathtub.'

Hanson looked over to Eva. She was all ears now, and a look of bewilderment passed between them. Hanson took another tack.

'So what of the truck driving?'

Leonid came back out of the fog. 'I am driving *kontrabanda* now. For Mafiya.' His eyes fell back directly on Hanson with the truth.

'What kind of contraband?' This from Eva.

'Now, vodka only. Before that, girls. Little heroin, too, but was most for girls.'

'These girls, where did they come from? Where did you work them?' Hanson grew animated.

'We work on E55. On *cheshskiy* side of border.'

'These were refugees, then? From Bosnia?'

'Many was. Yes.'

Hanson was beside himself. He told of encountering the issue back in '92 when he had been working out of Sarajevo: the growing problem of refugees in his camps in Croatia being spirited away by the Mafiya. He had tried desperately to put a stop to it, he said, sensing the disaster to come, a disaster on so many levels: widespread HIV infections across a continent; orphaned and abandoned children; the easy spread of hard drugs into Western Europe from the East; and, above all, a severe moral and spiritual decline. He had been unsuccessful in all his efforts. Now he sat, detained on a death watch, across from a representative of his nemesis. Three years down the road. Here he sat. How strange, he thought, and how amazing was this life. He felt no anger towards Leonid, only growing curiosity. Leonid had answers to questions that had plagued him since the

Bosnia days. He was happy now, just as he was always happy when riddles were solved. He forgot everything else, where he was and what would most likely happen the following day. He focused on Leonid.

He did understand that Leonid was only a henchman. He knew what it was to go hungry in Russia, and what Leonid's motivations most likely were. He had, after all, studied the problems of life in the post-Communist Bloc. It was a question of survival, nothing more. A man couldn't be blamed or held to account in such a situation. Could he?

Eva seemed to think he could. 'How did you manage to lure the girls into that sort of lifestyle, eh?' This in Russian.

'I didn't lure anyone. I just looked after them.'

'And dosed them up with drugs!'

'If they needed it, yes!'

Hanson looked on, anxiously. He couldn't understand any of it.

'You encouraged them to take the heroin, didn't you?'

'No! They were already hooked before I ever met them!'

'Your higher-ups saw to that, all right! Didn't they?'

'Listen, I was just a truck driver! It's got nothing to do with me if those girls were junkies! Stop trying to put it on me!'

'How do you look in the mirror, you son of a bitch!'

Leonid looked away from her, and turned back to Hanson. He couldn't argue any further, and so he switched back to broken English and began to tell the story of Galina, and the war criminal who had asked specifically for a Muslim. He spoke proudly of how Vlatsky had given the degenerate a sound trouncing. And then he ended by describing, bitterly, how he had cooked up her shot and given it to her. This version, although precise in its details, was morally imprecise. The story did have a villain, and juxtaposed with

116

him, Leonid somehow came out the hero when in reality he had been, at best, an ambivalent observer. What had he really done for Galina? Save her from having yet another traumatic experience with one man in one instance, while supervising her several hundred traumatic sexual experiences with a slew of other men? He encouraged her use of a drug that would only lead to premature annihilation, and even administered it to her. Why? Because it made her and the others easier to handle. And why do the job? So that he could get out of the shit and move to America. Could one really ever call him the hero of that story, or any other for that matter?

He had tears in his eyes after telling the story, though. He was remembering, as he spoke, of chasing the dragon day after day in Grozny. He thought of the mother and the daughter and the son. He thought of the wall that had come down on the son, how it had been his fault. Now he was losing it.

His telling of the tale of the E55 had a strong effect on both Hanson and Eva. Eva, for her part, decided to leave Leonid alone from now on. She understood his perspective. Good storytelling, effective storytelling, is not just about what you remember to put into it: it's also about what you remember to leave out. Leonid had left out whole tomes.

All three of them fell silent. They had their minds on other matters besides what would happen on the morrow, and although those matters could not necessarily be described as happy, they most certainly could be described as better; anything is better than contemplating your own murder throughout the long night.

❂

The Chechens, apparently, were going to drag this thing out. The following day, everything played out exactly as it had the day before. Graves were dug, weapons were aimed and guns were fired, but no one was killed. Two people slowly began losing their grip on sanity, just as the commander had predicted. Only one element was missing from the day's menu: Leonid was not tied to the tree or forced to watch, nor did he refill the empty graves. This time they left him in the same position that Hanson and Eva had suffered through. He waited in the room, not knowing their fate or his own. For a good five hours, he endured this torment before they were returned to him unharmed, and when they were, he knew that he would see another day.

Hanson, visibly strained, hugged him immediately upon entering the room. Eva touched his shoulder and sat in her corner, exhausted. A reversal was taking place between the two of them, Leonid noticed; Eva was bearing up better under the torture, a bit stronger now but perhaps only because she sensed Hanson weakening and felt it necessary to take the reins in hand herself. And weakening he was, which distressed Leonid as well.

Only moments after seating himself, Hanson launched into a flurried, overzealous monologue on the drastic necessity for Leonid to amend his life. Words spewed out of him at such a rate that the other two looked on, mouths agape. 'Here you are, Leonid, lost in Chechnya, far from your criminal background! You can start anew! You can reinvent yourself! Today!'

He began to use words, catchphrases of the NGO world usually used to describe natural disasters, to sum up Leonid's existence. 'Catastrophe, destructive by nature, in clearing out all pre-existing problems, in clearing the slate, allows us the opportunity to effect greater change!' he proclaimed.

Eva almost laughed at this. She might have, too, if she hadn't recognized in it something of surrender. Here was a great humanitarian, a man who had saved thousands, now taking on this pathetic little wretch as his next project, as if he knew that Leonid would be the last person to whom he would ever extend a helping hand.

Leonid found it bizarre at first, but soon warmed to Hanson's ideas. He realized now that his life was a shambles. The message was indeed getting through to him, that you could change your life and that the very best time, the most favourable time, was when you were down so low that you had nowhere else to go but up.

Hanson continued in this manner, throwing out vague ideas that were completely foreign to Leonid, concepts such as serving your fellow man. 'I know, I goddamn know you have it in you!' shrieked Hanson. Leonid nodded absently. 'You're Russian, you know the problems of the country. Hell, you've lived through them! Do it for your country! It needs all the help it can get!' Leonid nodded approvingly, dreaming again of immigrating to America.

Hanson's ramblings were beginning to sound more and more like a last will and testament to Eva's ears. He was already dead and gone, talking to the Russian as he would to a son from his deathbed. He was trying to save humankind from itself, trying to instil his own saintly humanity into – of all fucking people – Leonid. Eva thought of Hanson's actual son. She wondered how he would speak to him were he here instead of this cheap substitute. Then she thought of her daughter, and punched the wall.

She did not have the strength for this.

✿

Hanson and Eva were delivered back to Leonid the following day in less than perfect health. On top of the usual graveside festivities, the Chechens had reverted to the beating method. According to relative importance, Hanson had received the worst of it. Although Eva managed to walk back into the room by herself, Hanson was dumped on top of Leonid, completely unconscious. *Why are they always throwing him on top of me? Fucking dogs!*

'What the hell went on out there?'

'They seem to be tiring of our reluctance to confess. First it was beatings, then psychological torture and now both. What other tricks can they have left but to shoot us ...' Eva grunted this out. She was having trouble breathing. Leonid imagined gun butts working on her torso, bruising her ribs. Of this, he knew. Every pause in her speech, every breath taken expanding her lungs up against her ribcage, reminded him of the pain he had once experienced, the same pain the Frenchman back at the Royal Majestic must have known. Increasingly, the things in the present were making him think of the past, more than he ever had before. It was rendering him ill of heart.

A strange and haunting music drifted through to them from under the door, played on a cassette deck at high volume. It consisted of a powerful, rhythmic stamping of many, many feet, punctuated by deep grunting and the ecstatic chanting of what sounded like passages from the

Qur'an. They could hear the name of God rising above the stamping: *'Allah! ... Allah!'* The rhythm would intensify into a frenzied jackhammering of feet, then ebb, then resume. All the while, the chanting, by a single voice, provided a counterpoint. The effect was hypnotic.

Centuries of Russian rule had resulted in a tolerance for alcohol amongst the Chechens; now, mingled with the music, came the unmistakable sounds of men drinking together. It was the first time Leonid and Eva had heard their captors listening to music or drinking, and it struck Eva, in particular, dead. It didn't mean *nothing* – nothing meant *nothing*. These two things combined definitely meant something.

'I know that they will kill us soon,' Eva told Leonid, something she could never say to Hanson. 'I'm sure that they will murder us tomorrow.' She looked at him hard, her lips trembling.

Being unskilled at consolation, all Leonid could come up with was: 'Of course they won't. Why should they? Don't be ridiculous.'

Eva understood that she could never get what she needed at the moment from him, and retreated into her corner, turning away from Leonid. Meanwhile, Leonid was struggling to get Hanson off him; as he did so, he noticed, for the first time, that Hanson wore a ring with an odd design. He stopped what he was doing in order to examine it more closely. It was an alphabet he did not recognize, and he remarked that Hanson wore it on the left hand and on his wedding ring finger. It was made of brass, and although it had clearly been falling apart – pieces of the filigreed ornamentation had broken off – its simple beauty still held Leonid's eye. He wanted to know more about it.

He addressed Eva: 'Do you know what this says here, on his ring?'

'No. I'm a Russian–English translator. Sanskrit doesn't exactly enter into it,' she replied sarcastically, though with a tremor in her voice.

'Sanskrit! I didn't know Hanson was a Hindu.'

Eva laughed and softened a bit. 'He's Presbyterian! Only a kid like you could make him into a Hindu!'

'Well it's on his fucking marriage finger!'

'He's not married. He's twice divorced.'

'So what's the meaning?'

'I have no idea. It's something he likes to fiddle with.'

'What does that mean?'

'I just noticed him twisting and turning it on his finger. Always playing with it. Especially in stressful times.'

The music in the other room rose a few decibels, bringing Eva's dark thoughts back to the forefront. The Chechens were getting drunker.

'So you don't know anything more about it?' Leonid continued.

'Will you fuck off with your stupid questions! Bill is not a Hindu!' She barked.

Thus reproached, Leonid returned to the task of removing the American from him. Eva watched him rearrange Hanson's beleaguered body into a spot off to the side. She watched the scene in horror, as if observing an alien moving a human corpse. Leonid handled him so awkwardly – had he never touched another person before? Was it loathsome to him? Eva decided he was a Martian. Exhausted, her nerves shot, she fell asleep with this thought.

✿

They were allowed to sleep in the next day, as their captors remained passed out late into the afternoon from the carrying-on of the previous night. Of the three prisoners, only one would require rousing, and that was Hanson. He was still unconscious from his beating. Both Leonid and Eva thought he might have died, but a swift Chechen kick to the ribs proved them wrong. Hanson got to his feet, but he wasn't really there anymore.

They were all dragged out to the usual place, in their usual roles. Eva took the reintroduction of Leonid into the game as yet another very bad sign. He was put by the tree, but remained untied. The other two were forced to their knees before the pair of deep holes they had dug two days earlier. They did not plead with their assassins, nor did they even try and console one another. They were broken now.

In an instant, Hanson was dead, face-down in his grave. Eva was given but the briefest of chances to answer for her crimes, a gun barrel pushed up to the back of her skull.

'Are you CIA!' As ever, it wasn't a question.

Instead of answering them, she spoke to Leonid in English, without looking back at him. She answered to his fear, forgetting her own: 'Because they are showing you this, you will survive.'

Then there was a muted crack, and she fell into her pit.

The Chechen soldiers trod off, bleary-eyed. Only one stayed back. He thrust a shovel into Leonid's hands and motioned towards the holes. Leonid began filling Eva's grave first, taking his time throwing the dirt over her while pondering her last words. He decided to put no faith in them. *I am next.* Her words were as empty as her dead eyes, as empty as the path through her skull and brain that the bullet had cleared before exiting through her right cheek.

He was about a quarter of the way through the filling when his guard began vomiting. It didn't last long – a few mere heaves and he was alright again. The soldier scooped up some fresh snow and buried his tearing eyeballs and runny nose in it while Leonid watched. He let the heat coming off his forehead melt the rest of it and only lowered his hands to face Leonid again when it was all gone. Then he gestured with his Kalashnikov that Leonid should get back to work.

As he continued working on Eva's grave, Leonid reflected on how long it had been since he had needed to revive himself as the soldier had. How wretched the man appeared to him – and how wretched he himself must previously have been. For despite all his current and rather dire worries, it flashed in his head that he never wanted to find himself sick like that, booze-sick, ever again. He'd been sober for quite a while now and, as much as his circumstances normally would have dictated that he be definitely in need of a shnort, he felt he didn't want one.

By the time Leonid had covered Eva completely, the soldier had thrown up twice more. This, to him, signified that it was time for a little hair of the dog. The soldier pulled out a flask and had himself a nice, long shot. *By a fucking alcoholic, I'm gonna get killed! This isn't fair! By alcoholism I should be killed, not like this!*

Leonid began working on Hanson's grave. Hanson had fallen in awkwardly, with his left arm behind his back. As Leonid shovelled, and as the dirt rose around the body, his eye caught sight of that ring again. There it was, barely shiny anymore. Leonid decided impulsively that he must have it, that it had mystical properties and could save him.

He looked over to the Chechen. His head was tilted back towards the heavens as he took another swig. Leonid threw his spade into the grave and dove in after it. Quickly, he pried the ring off and put it on his own finger, while crying out for help. As he waited for the hung-over soldier to lift him out of the pit, he noticed something that scared the hell out of him: Hanson's finger, where the ring had been, was coloured a deathly green. He was so spooked by this that he hardly noticed the soldier reaching down, offering his hand. Leonid, ignorant of the fact that a brass ring will stain human skin after much wear, had the impression that Hanson was decomposing at an incredibly fast rate.

He was out of the grave now, and panting heavily. The guard took pity on him and offered up his flask: 'Here, take a hit.'

Leonid's new inclination to teetotalling of a moment ago was revealed for the nonsense it was. He automatically reached out for the flask, and drank deeply. At once refreshed and lucid from the jolt, he asked, without fear: 'Will they kill me next?'

Only a swine would counter such an honest question with mendacity, especially with a drinking partner. 'Most certainly,' the soldier said simply. 'Once you've got these two buried.'

❂

'No, no! God, no!' Leonid was on his knees, and the Kalashnikov was shoved up against the back of his own head. But this time there was no ceremony, no grave digging, no melodramatic threats, no demands for a confession. This was going to be a straight-up, no-holds-barred execution.

The gun was on him, and nothing short of a miracle was going to stop it going off.

Leonid thought hard. It suddenly came to him to mention Borzoi's name, in a last-ditch effort to save his skin. He yelled it out, though no one was asking of him anything more than his quick demise. Borzoi's name alone, however, was enough to lessen the gravity of the situation, and Leonid immediately sensed that.

The commander scoffed: 'Everybody knows of Borzoi. Give me another name, now!'

Now, for an alcoholic to remember a tiny shred of information overheard at a party while in the middle of a world-class binge, a miracle is exactly how you'd have to describe what happened next.

Leonid had a moment of total recall. His last night in Moscow at the Royal Majestic came back to him, vividly. He was on his way to the toilets. He passed by Miki and Borzoi. Borzoi gestured towards him and said: '_____ will look after him.' Leonid understood that only that name could save him. He strained to get that name back.

'Hurry up!'

He let himself feel the cold gunmetal on his head, and the small circle it described, in an effort to scare his memory into kicking in. And it did. The whispered name returned to Leonid.

It was like honey on his tongue. The name of the Chechen, Borzoi's connection, the one he and Miki had spoken of while laughing at him, at how they were setting him up. Now that he had that name back, he would never forget it again.

A finger was squeezing back on the trigger just as Leonid pronounced the name softly. The Chechen's ears pricked up in recognition as his gun fell limply down from Leonid's head.

For the name he had uttered was not an actual name, but the very secret alias of a high-ranking Chechen fighter known only to them. This man, a scourge to the Russians, held hero status and godlike power over the hearts and minds of the Chechen people.

'What!? Say that again!' screamed the commander.

Leonid repeated the name, and then continued: 'I'm here, in Chechnya, as a go-between for Borzoi and him. A middleman, here on business.'

'So what were you doing in the middle of the countryside, looking all fucked up?'

'The Russians. We got caught in the bombing, in Grozny. They killed my partner. I'm lucky to be alive.' He lied dumbly, automatically, as if in a trance – or drunk.

'Why didn't you tell us all this earlier?'

'Because who the hell knows what's going on in this fucking country? Who knows who is on whose side, and who might be an enemy? I'm at my wits' end, fuck!' With this, he collapsed on the ground, sobbing like a trained thespian even as relief swept over him. For he knew, all bets were off on his execution. They would not be killing him. Not anymore.

Nor would they be aiding his repatriation, he found out later over some drinks. He was free to go, but they wouldn't help him on this one, not with the war still raging. He was free – but it was turning out to be the kind of freedom people only think they want.

Leonid asked for a smoke with his vodka. They handed him one, along with a big box of matches – which he pocketed surreptitiously. He was becoming good at this survival stuff.

Night had come, and it was cold outside. These were the circumstances under which they loosed him. He'd much rather have stayed with them until morning, but dared not ask. They were a grim crew, and as the drinking began anew, they were growing grimmer.

'You may now go,' said the commander. 'Your friends are our friends.' He turned up the now-familiar music.

'Right now?' whispered Leonid.

'Of course not!' shouted a large, bearded soldier. 'First another drink, then you go!' He refilled Leonid's glass with more vodka. *Probably* my *fucking vodka ... bastards!*

Glasses were clinked and *nostrovyas* were called out all around the room. They drank.

'Good luck on your journey,' the commander said, soullessly and without conviction. 'You go ... now!' With that, he motioned towards the door.

Leonid remained seated. He decided to take a chance. In a tremulous voice, he said: 'Why end the party so early? Let's have a few more.'

'You sound scared. Are you scared, Leonid?'

'Why should I be scared? You wouldn't kill your friend's friend, right?'

'No,' the commander replied slowly, 'but I might kill my enemy's enemy.' Leonid nearly hoarked.

'Why would you do that, comrade? Your enemy's enemy is your friend, no?'

The commander drew his pistol and aimed it squarely at Leonid. 'We've had our drink, and now you are overstaying your welcome. Leave ... you Russian dog!'

Leonid was beyond arguing. He stood up on shaky legs and went straight for the door.

'Hey, Leonid!' the bearded soldier shouted after him, cocking his gun. 'Don't worry! You won't die!'

As the soldiers laughed raucously behind him, Leonid broke into a jog, the memory of that expression haunting him. Breathing hard, he awaited the punchline. The commander fired a shot above his head for punctuation's sake, and delivered it without mirth: 'You'll see!'

Leonid sprinted through the woods, away from the laughter and into the dark.

Eight

It soon seemed to Leonid that he had walked the length and breadth of the small republic. Realizing that the ground beneath him was steadily inclining, he decided against tackling the Caucasian mountaintops. Knowing them to be south of his position finally gave him true north. It was, as always, Ingushetia in the west that he wanted to reach. He pointed his toes in what he considered to be a northerly direction and, after ten long days of walking, came out of the war zone and into western Dagestan. He hadn't bothered with shelter and all that this time; he just kept moving, eating what he could and building fires at night. Stopping for any length of time was not an option, and when he did arrive, he was wretched.

❂

That was how he came to be living in a refugee camp, in one of a long line of railway boxcars that had fallen into disrepair. He had neighbours now, too, all of them fleeing the war next door. Way back in January, when he and Spaska had driven into Grozny, some of these very same people had been walking in the other direction, carrying all they could, prophesying the hell to come.

Given the underworld they had come from, the residents had made the camp a remarkably normal place. Clothes were hung out to dry on lines running between cars, which seemingly tied the whole community together. All the cooking smells you'd expect invaded the nostrils around mealtimes. The once-again joyful screams of children were accompanied by the grunts of adults busy at work. In short, it presented a scene of ordinary small-town life. Even though it was a refugee camp, nothing lent it a hint of dispossession. Nothing really, except for the wheels on those boxcars.

Another thing stood out to make one think of small-town life, and that was the air of hospitality. Yet again, Leonid was profiting from the kindness of strangers. Unlike them, he had arrived with nothing. Seeing that, acknowledging that, they gave him everything. They put him above their own wants. They took him in as one of their own, and although most of them were ethnic Chechens, they were all united by their status as refugees.

He had arrived twisted, bent and emaciated, and slowly, little by little, they undid the damage. They cared for him in a way that even his own father hadn't, since childhood. He felt at home again, a feeling that had been lost to him since well before he'd ever put a foot on Chechen soil.

Leonid befriended an ethnic Russian named Dudi, a gentle giant of a man. It was he who had first understood Leonid's babbling when he'd emerged from the woods. The Dagestanis and Chechens and Georgians and Ukrainians who had helped, dragging the near-senseless Leonid out of the cold and into their warmth, could not understand him. Dudi did, however, and not because of dialect or language; what Dudi understood was trauma. He'd seen much of it.

Most of Leonid's talk was rambling and incoherent at that point. He mentioned things in odd, surreal ways. He said, for example, that a group of bears had tried to murder him with their guns so that they might have him for their breakfast. He asked if there were any exploding televisions around. He said he had a magical ring.

Everyone at the camp had seen this type of disorientation many times before. It was nothing new to them; some had even come out of this kind of shock themselves, with help. So they helped him. They unbent him. And slowly, he became part of the community – a functioning part, even.

One day, Dudi asked Leonid if he was married.

'Of course not,' Leonid replied. 'Why do you ask?'

'That ring on your finger, the "magic" one.' He laughed.

Leonid hadn't even realized it himself until then, but he had put Hanson's ring on his wedding-ring finger, exactly as Hanson himself had worn it. He hadn't even thought of it at all for weeks, so distracted had he been with simply surviving. No, not since after he snapped and started talking to the damn thing, asking it for directions and continually coming up empty.

He played with it, moving the ring up and down his digit thoughtfully, not even aware of the sexual connotations of this gesture. He was shocked to discover that his finger, where the ring had been, had turned green. Again, just like Hanson. He shivered. *Hanson had this colour after they killed him. Maybe it's contagious. Maybe it is magic. Dark magic!*

He snapped out of it and finally answered Dudi: 'This is just a memento.'

'Of what? If you don't mind me asking.'

'Some people who died, back in Chechnya.'

'I'm sorry. Were they friends? Family?'

'Neither, actually.' Leonid paused to think on that. 'They were more like teachers, I suppose.'

'How did they die?'

'They were executed. Shot in the back of the head, right in front of me.' Leonid said this with a faraway look.

'Executed! Were they important people?'

'One was American. A relief worker. This was his ring. The other was his translator. A Georgian woman. They were accused of being KGB or FSB or CIA or some ridiculous thing. The Chechens made me bury them.' Leonid was surprised, hearing himself revealing things to Dudi so easily.

'That's horrible! No wonder you were so spooked when we found you!'

'Yes, no wonder ...' Leonid paused again before continuing. 'I think, sometimes, that through their deaths, they somehow saved my life.'

'How?'

'Really, I don't know. But the translator, the Georgian woman, told me that I would survive because I was witnessing the death of this great American. It made no sense to me at the time, but now, when I look back on it, I can't argue with the logic of her statement.'

Leonid wasn't quite sure why he was lying his ass out like this; he knew damn well that his knowledge of the secret name of a Chechen warlord was the only thing that had come between him and a cold ditch. The Chechens hadn't given a good goddamn what he'd witnessed or what its significance was; they would have killed him for the hell of it, one way or another. Still, Leonid corrupted the story further, overtaken by a mystical zeal.

'I think she meant that it was destined to be ...' He stared at Hanson's ring as he mumbled this. He'd stopped playing with it.

'What bullshit!' Dudi exclaimed. 'Clearly, she was in shock. There is not a bit of reality in what you say. Perhaps she was trying to immortalize herself by saving you, or rather by claiming to save you! We call that a messiah complex!'

'You weren't there, Dudi! You don't understand what passed between us. All three of us!' Leonid said this with such vehemence that Dudi backed off and brought the debate down a couple of notches.

'You're right, OK, I wasn't there, but I have met many people under duress. Sometimes they say strange things, it's only natural. Hell, you should have heard the crap coming out of your mouth when we first found you! What were you eating out in those woods anyways, magic mushrooms?'

'What are you trying to say?'

'Just that you were talking crazy.'

'I don't mean that. I meant before.'

'Oh, that. You say there was logic to her statement. What logic? She was about to be murdered – you survived. Fine. That's not because they died. In war, everything is random! You might as well apply your logic and your destiny to throwing dice!'

After that, they both fell silent. But Leonid still felt something was afoot, something that Dudi would not, could not acknowledge.

✿

After some time, a relief agency, having somehow heard about the makeshift camp and the conditions the people there were living under, organized some aid for them. But things being what they were in the world of NGOs, and the bureaucrats within them and without, the process of actually helping people was maddeningly slow.

When help finally did arrive, a great change came over the camp. The displaced were moved out of the boxcars and into heated tents (though some chose to stay behind, feeling the cars to be rather homey now). Proper latrines were dug, instead of everyone simply going off into the woods to do their business (yet many returned to the woods afterwards, preferring them to the great stench). They no longer had to forage or hunt for food (but the heartier ones still did). Three meals a day were served up (although those could only be described as gruel). They now had medicine, a doctor and two nurses to look after their health (yet the older ones stuck to their own remedies anyway). And so, life became a little bit lighter.

Leonid watched these transformations with his eyes wide open. Often, he would think of Hanson, and how he might have devised the schematics of the camp – probably, he imagined, with a much higher degree of efficiency. He also thought of Eva: he saw her translating, keeping the flow of communication between people running smoothly. And denigrating him, of course.

As he watched the camp evolve around him, remarking on the mistakes being made, he grew more contemplative – yet his depression also deepened. Observing pieces falling into place and the process by which that happened, he experienced a strong sense of what had been lost in the murders of Hanson and Eva. Not a personal loss but a public one, perhaps even a global loss.

Yet for all the positive approaches to life that Hanson had tried to drive into Leonid, he still succumbed to despair at the shape of the world, and the more he did so, the more he caved in on himself. Whereas before he wouldn't have cared enough to notice, now he noticed that he was starting to care.

Leonid sat alone atop a railway car one night, watching an electrical storm in the distance, a spectacle of lightning that illuminated the forest below and the low-lying clouds above for brief moments. There was no thunder to be heard. Leonid just stared and stared. The storm was coming towards him, he saw, and he knew it might be dangerous to be up this high on a metal surface. Yet he didn't move. He understood that whatever was coming for him was going to come, one way or the other.

And it came, and then it went, and Leonid was still alive.

For several weeks, a van had been driving in and around Chechnya. The people within were mostly American, and they were asking detailed questions everywhere they stopped – a most dangerous undertaking in the region, a mission verging on suicide; yet they were not bothered by Russian indifference or Chechen threats. Their questions pertained to a certain Bill Hanson. It was a search party, and the group included one very special participant: Hanson's son, George.

On the hundred and third day after Hanson's disappearance, they arrived at Leonid's refugee camp and, as they had been doing everywhere, showed Hanson's photo around and asked questions. Were it not for Dudi, the forlorn group might never have encountered Leonid, who was off in the woods taking one of his half-hour shits.

George had all but abandoned the quest for his father by the time he arrived at this camp. Everyone from lowlife Russian and American officials to lowlife Mafiya types had advised him to give up, and he was more than half ready to do just that. George didn't expect to find his father alive after such a long a time. He only wanted his body and a proper burial Stateside: this is what he told people, and it was a viable excuse to be putting himself and others in harm's way. During the downtime, though, when he wasn't out searching, when he found himself alone in some dank room late at night, unable to sleep, he burned with one sole desire: he wanted to *know*. He wanted the story of his father's disappearance. He wanted the mystery solved.

Then he met Dudi, who persuaded him, through a translator, to wait a little longer before leaving. He told George that he was almost one hundred percent certain that a friend of his in the camp had known his father: 'Give me five minutes, I'll bring you Leonid.'

Leonid, having just finished dutifully leaf-wiping his ass, was pulling up his trousers when he heard someone calling out his name. Dudi ran up to him and anxiously pushed and pulled Leonid towards the people in the van.

'What's the excitement? Where are you rushing me?' Leonid kept asking Dudi such questions and, getting no reply, kept pulling back. Dudi was making him nervous, putting his back up.

'Just come, already!' Dudi screamed at him.

Leonid gradually came towards the people who required the information that only he possessed: the final resting places of Hanson and Eva. George began the questioning half-heartedly. He'd been led on wild goose chases dozens of times by that point, and had little faith left. He held up the photo. 'Do you recognize this man?'

Leonid was shocked. He had tried to put the entire experience of his Chechen captivity out of his mind. It only caused him to feel a dull, senseless guilt, which he didn't ever want to explore. *Who the hell is this guy?*

The translator began, but Leonid cut him off: 'Who you are?'

'You speak English,' George Hanson said. 'Good. Do you know this man?'

'Who you are?' Leonid repeated.

'Just answer the question, please!'

George showing him that photograph made Leonid feel as though he were under investigation for some crime, and George's tone and language didn't help, either. So he lied: 'I do not know of this person,' he said, waving the picture away.

George raised his shoulders and looked at Dudi, then turned to his companions: 'Have we gone all around the camp?' The answer came back affirmative. 'Then let's get going. Another dead end, another waste of time. Come on.' With that, the group sauntered off back to their van.

Dudi couldn't understand what had just transpired. Even though he had no English, Leonid's rigidity told him everything. 'What the hell are you doing?' he said.

He received only an aloof, faraway look. He shook Leonid, but nothing changed; Leonid stared as though in a trance.

Dudi decided to act. He picked up Leonid like a child, threw him over his shoulder and hurried over to the van just as the engine ignited. Leonid did not resist. Dudi banged urgently on the passenger side window – George's window – and when it rolled down, Dudi grabbed his friend's hand and thrust it forward so that George might inspect it more closely. George looked at it blandly, not understanding, but seconds later his sleep-deprived eyes went ablaze, rekindled first by grief, then by anger.

He kicked his door open, knocking both Dudi and Leonid down to the muddy ground. George got on top of Leonid and pinned his arms to the ground with his knees. He grabbed him by the hair and threatened him with a fist, screaming wildly: 'Where in fuck did you get that, you miserable fucking wretch? Where!'

Leonid did not reply.

'Tell me right now! Where did you get my father's ring from, you son of a bitch!' George drew out a hunting knife from a sheath on his belt and held it under Leonid's chin.

Still nothing.

Dudi tried prying George off Leonid and received a slash to the forearm for his trouble. George's people were all out of the van now, trying to restrain him. He couldn't hear or even see them. He was beside himself, in a kind of tango to the death with Leonid, whom he evidently assumed was his father's murderer. Leonid, being the cheating woman in the dance, dared not speak.

George pressed the tip of the blade against Leonid's chin, making his point – and its own – felt. He demanded again to know where the ring came from. Leonid remained mute. A bead of blood appeared on his chin, and threatened to become a rivulet.

Dudi, kneeling by Leonid, screamed at him to speak, to say something, anything.

'Where's my father, you murdering thief!'

Leonid had a brief flash of his walk in the woods with his grandfather as a child. It lasted a split second, but brought him out of his trance. He looked directly into George's eyes and spoke calmly, evenly: 'Your father gave me ring before execution.'

'Who? By who! Who killed him, goddamit?'

Leonid said only one word more, and then George fell off him and began to weep violently, rolling around in the muck and mire. All Leonid had said was: 'Chechens.'

Look at this, I'm living in luxury! thought Leonid as they drove through the Chechen countryside towards Ingushetia. Most people wouldn't consider being tossed about in the back of a van speeding along bumpy roads as luxurious, but then most people hadn't spent the past couple of months living as Leonid had done.

George now had everything he'd really wanted – the true story – and Leonid had given it to him, chapter and verse. All that was left to do was to retrieve his father's corpse. That was what they were attempting now, by driving into Chechnya.

They had made a deal, George and Leonid, and part of that deal, beyond the retrieval of the body, was the return of Hanson's ring. George wore it now, leaving Leonid's finger naked once again. When he had returned it, he'd asked George what the writing on it meant.

'It's a short Buddhist prayer for peace and compassion. It reads: *Om mani padme hum.* My father bought it in India back in the Sixties. He hasn't taken it off since, not even to wash his hands. He believed, my father did, that everything was connected to everything else.' George had grown weepy. 'Can you understand that? Are you capable?'

After hearing this short story behind the ring, Leonid believed he was indeed capable. He also wished it was still his. By way of keeping it, he repeated the words in his head, trying to memorize them: *Om mani padme hum.*

In the van, along for the ride, were Phil, an American NGO officer who had worked under Bill Hanson; Conrad, a representative from the American embassy in Moscow; and sitting beside George, who was driving, the translator, who was named Spaska. Leonid couldn't believe it when the introductions were made. Certainly, it was a bad portent. *My poor, dead friend. You look different, but it is you, isn't it? Have you come back to haunt me? What do you want of me?*

Leonid had explained the Chechens' assertion that Hanson and Eva were spies – FSB or CIA, it didn't really matter much. George wanted to know what had led the Chechens to that notion. More importantly, he wanted to know who had led his father up there. In his mind, it had clearly been a setup, and his prime suspects were the Russians – though he had others in mind, too, someone in the US government, perhaps. He told Leonid that, over the years, some of his father's actions in the field had gone against US foreign policy, and that he had made some powerful enemies as a result. But George preferred not to dwell on this fact; his father had also made some powerful friends. In any case, he first had to move his father's status from 'missing' to a confirmed 'killed'. He was told the only way to achieve this other than through the sufficient passage of time was to retrieve a corpse.

'That asshole at the embassy actually had the stones to tell me that it would be preferable if a bullet or two were embedded in the body. The shithead!'

'He shouldn't have said that,' Conrad replied. 'I already told you, I'm sorry. He's just not that good with people.'

'Whatever. Maybe I'll kick him in his cunt when we get back.'

Leonid looked up, puzzled. '"Cunt"? How possible for man to have cunt?'

'You're a funny guy, Leonid,' said Phil.

They all chuckled, except for Spaska. He couldn't understand it either.

Despite Leonid's sincerest affirmations that he had not a clue as to the location of the shack where he had been held with Hanson and Eva – that he'd been brought there with a sack over his head – George forged ahead. The younger Hanson insisted that it could only have been in a handful of locations, what with Chechnya being so small and George knowing the lay of the land after three weeks traversing it. They also knew the general route his father had taken the day that he'd gone missing, which further narrowed the odds of finding him.

Although months had passed and most of the country's landscape had been remodelled through the art of bombardment, George was sure the shack would not have been disturbed by the constant shelling.

'But it was falling apart,' Leonid argued, 'just like these we are passing. All look the same!'

'We'll find it. I know we will.'

'And soldiers? Could still be there. Kill us dead, no problem!'

'They won't be there. They'd have moved by now. Besides, we have a deal – or did you forget already?'

That shut Leonid up. If this worked out, his dream of America would be a dream no longer.

But Phil was getting nervous, too: 'I don't know, George. Leonid could have a point here. We'd better tread lightly ...'

George ignored them both. He was on a mission. There was every good reason to stop the search, call the whole thing off. Yet he insisted on pushing through: 'We start looking around tomorrow, and that's that.'

They went 'looking around' for a period of seven days. What occurred on the eighth day persuaded George to stop the search. It also persuaded him to never set foot in Chechnya again.

❁

The group checked in to a hostel in Arshti, Ingushetia, in which Bill Hanson had last been seen. They would base themselves there. It was Leonid's first decent accommodation in months. It even had a phone, which made him realize he hadn't communicated with anyone in Moscow since Miki's party, not even his father. Still, it was late by the time they pulled in; he decided to put off contact for another time. He also needed to think of what he was going to say to Miki. *Goddamn bastard.*

'Anyone want a nightcap?' George asked, ordering a beer from the woman who ran the place.

'Yes, yes!' Leonid pushed ahead of the others and requested a bottle of vodka.

'Take it easy, man. We leave at seven-thirty in the AM.'

'Not for worry on me. Just kick me in head, I am ready.'

'When was the last time you took a drink?' asked George. 'I imagine it's been awhile.' Leonid remembered his last taste with the Chechens. 'You better share that with Spaska,' George added. 'He's a vodka man. That much might get right on top of you.'

'OK, OK. You are the winner. Come, Spaska, we drink. Will be like old times.'

Spaska couldn't fathom the meaning of this comment, which the Americans simply interpreted as a Russian expression of some sort.

'Mind if I tag along?' asked Conrad. 'I'm not quite ready for bed yet.'

'Not at all,' Spaska replied. 'Come and sit with us.'

Leonid was slightly annoyed by Spaska's invitation. He wanted some one-on-one time with this ghost. He had serious questions that needed answering.

The three of them and the bottle all sat at an outdoor table. Leonid started in right away with the drinking. He'd decided to speak only in Russian in order to cut Conrad out of the conversation. 'That's a strange name for a Russian, "Spaska", I mean,' he said. 'It's not even a real name, is it?'

'It's a nickname. My grandmother started calling me this when I was a baby. She was senile at the time.'

'She'd have to have been! It's a ridiculous name.'

'Well it's stuck with me all these years. I'm quite fond of it.'

'Come on! What's your real name, for Christ's sake?' Leonid was becoming agitated.

'My given names are Sergei Danilovich.'

'That's better. We'll call you that from now on.'

Conrad jumped in here, revealing fluent Russian: 'I like Spaska's nickname. Why do you have such a hard time with it?'

Leonid jumped in his chair. *A fucking spy, they sent!* 'Slooshy! He is speaking Russian!'

'Of course. It's a job requirement. I work at the embassy, remember? So why do you hate his name so much?'

'No, is personal.' Leonid turned back to Spaska. 'You know, I used to know a Spaska. You are like him, only less … how should I say it … less retarded.'

'You're flattering me now.' Spaska took a drink through smirking lips. 'So where is this retarded twin of mine?'

'He's dead. He was killed in Grozny.'

'Easy place for that to happen.'

'Come on, Spaska,' Leonid said, suddenly extremely uneasy. 'Admit it to me! There can't be two people with a name like that! Even in all of Russia!'

'Admit what?'

Conrad nearly fell out of his chair with laughter. 'He thinks you're a ghost! A fucking apparition!'

Spaska started laughing too. Leonid turned red, and took a very long pull of vodka. 'Fuck the both of you!' He drank some more, then rose from his chair and towered over Spaska. 'Come on, Spaska, leave Sergei alone. Get out of there.'

This only made the other men laugh harder. Leonid began shaking Spaska, trying to oust the spirit of the other Spaska from Sergei's body. 'Get lost, you idiot! Go back to Hell, where you belong! You're going to get us all killed up here, you son of a bitch! Sergei! Sergei! Can you hear me in there? Push Spaska out. Push! Like a baby! Or a shit! Just *push!*'

Now Spaska and Conrad were convulsing with hilarity. Leonid gave up his efforts at exorcism. He grabbed the remains of the bottle and walked off to his room, muttering under his breath. 'You'll see. You'll see. As Jesus said: "Those who laugh now will cry later." You dogs! Just wait. You'll see!'

❂

Day Eight began like any other in Arshti, with a quick, shitty little breakfast, a short poring-over of the local maps, loading up the van with provisions and vodka for Leonid, plus the three shovels, two picks and two body bags George and his group had brought. Then off they went, back across the border into Chechnya after seven unsuccessful trips over as many days.

Leonid, however, was growing more and more reluctant with each new sortie, his fear of Spaska's ghost as unrelenting as his fear of the Chechens. But the deal he had made with George was one he simply had to take. It was he, after all, who had suggested it, and George had taken it up a notch. Leonid had told him of his dream of living in America; George had told him that for his troubles, he would not only take him to the US, but would arrange for speedy citizenship through his connections at the State Department (really, his father's). In addition to this, George would provide him with a monthly stipend until such time as Leonid could support himself. These bargaining chips plus the vodka ensured that Leonid got in that van each and every day. He could already taste the Pizza Hut.

A roadblock ahead observed, everyone tightened up. They had been through countless checkpoints like these, but their reactions were always the same, always tense. Spaska slowed down and eased up to the soldiers. Leonid, apprehensive, could scarcely control himself. In full flashback mode he began whisper-yelling in Russian: 'Spaska, you fucking idiot! Ram through! Ram through! Are you trying to get me killed again?'

'Who are you calling an idiot? Shut up! They're coming to the window!'

It was a Chechen roadblock, not a Russian one: Spaska was relieved. The Russians were clearly trying to dissuade outsiders from visiting this unpopular war. At a Russian checkpoint, a journalist could be detained for hours, even days. At a Chechen checkpoint, one could easily be waved through. Or then again, simply shot. Either way, you'd have your answer without any dilly-dallying.

Spaska rolled down the window and said: 'Hello ...'

'Hello?' came the reply. 'Where the fuck do you think you are? Get out of the van! Everybody, out of the van and down on the ground! Lie flat on your stomachs!'

The doors were flung open by Chechen soldiers, hostility carved into their brows. Guns were pointed and shirts were grabbed. Spaska, frozen with fear, began – too late – to translate the instructions for the Americans. But there was no need: everybody understood anyway.

Lying face-down on the muddy roadside, they were all frisked. Although the soldiers confiscated George's hunting knife, the only weapon in the group, it was really money they were looking for. They found quite a bit of that, too.

The soldiers spoke hurriedly amongst themselves and made decisions loudly and excitedly before finally addressing the group: 'Everyone back in the van. You will follow our vehicle. These two' – the speaker indicated a couple of the soldiers – 'will ride with you. Come, quickly! Get up! Let's go!'

Spaska translated, trying to put a positive spin on the situation, but no one was fooled. Anxiously, they all got back into the van, followed by the two heavily armed Chechens.

Taking the wheel, Spaska followed the Chechen armoured personnel carrier a few miles down the main road until it turned off and took a heavily wooded and narrow dirt track. He paused and looked to the others. George's eyes were communicating something he understood perfectly, and agreed with: *We don't want to go in there.*

The Chechen guards in back began to shout: 'Come on, move it! Keep going!' They were screaming into Leonid's ear and aiming their weapons past his head at Spaska. Leonid's head swam with visions from the last few months. He saw a chance and took it like a man demonically possessed. *Om mani padme fuck!*

He jumped over the back seat and furiously attacked both of the soldiers with his fists, miraculously even managing to overwhelm them for several moments. Phil quickly joined the romp, and George got out of the front seat, opened up the back of the van and pitched into the beating.

The embassy rep, Conrad, shook helplessly in his seat. Spaska kept an eye on the APC. It was backing up the narrow track with difficulty; there was no room to turn around. 'Hurry! The others are coming back!' he shouted.

One of the soldiers in the back managed get a finger on his trigger, and fired a round off. Blood sprayed all over the interior of the van. Spaska too, was covered in it.

Leonid looked up. *Not again, Spaska! Jesus Christ!*

Phil screamed: 'Shit! They got Conrad!' The embassy official lay across the seat, dead. Dead and faceless.

Leonid called out: 'Spaska!'

But Spaska was still alive. 'Let's go,' he shouted, 'they're almost here!'

The three men in back were invigorated by the sight of the blood. They wanted to see more of it now. George pulled the gun out of the shooter's hand and shot him twice in the stomach.

'That's for my father and Eva!' More blood filled the van. He pushed the wounded soldier out the back while the other two continued to beat their man.

'Drive, Spaska! Go!' George ordered, and then he shot the wounded man on the ground, in the head. As the van sped away, he called out to the corpse: 'And that's for Conrad!'

'What do we do with this guy?' asked Phil, referring to the now-unconscious Chechen soldier.

'We keep him for insurance. Let's see what the APC does.'

They were too far ahead now for the APC to catch up to them. It still hadn't even completely backed out of the track.

The van headed back towards the checkpoint, where their troubles had begun; the only difference was that they now had weapons, two pistols and two Kalashnikovs. As most of the checkpoint guards had gone off with the group, there remained only two at the blockade. George had a plan.

He opened the sliding door on the right side of the van and held the hostage guard in front of him as a shield, while randomly firing his pistol at the two men at their post. Leonid fired one of the Kalashnikovs awkwardly from the same side. The other two shot out the left side.

Spaska drove through at full speed. The Chechens returned fire, but only managed to ding the van and break some windows. They didn't even come close to shooting their own guy. As soon as they were through, George pushed his pistol into the hostage's spine and blew a hole right through the middle of him. The body fell out the open door onto the road and bounced a few times, as though the man was a mere rubbish sack.

Leonid jumped at the shot and turned to look at George. Phil was looking at him, too. George wore no trace of remorse on his face, just a look of almost post-orgasmic serenity.

The Chechens had no vehicle, and could not give chase. Still, Spaska drove furiously until they were all safely back in Arshti.

●

'How the hell am I gonna explain this to the embassy?' said George as he quaffed another beer. They who had survived Day Eight sat around the outdoor table at their hostel. 'Maybe it's our fault. Maybe we overreacted.' He looked directly at Leonid as he said this, which did not go unnoticed.

'You want maybe go back? We go! Come!' Leonid shouted. 'In all cases, I warned you not to go. Now you see.' Leonid remembered Spaska and Conrad laughing at him. *I know a ghost when I see one, God damn them! They should have listened to me! Idiots!*

Spaska intervened: 'They were going to kill us, George. There is no doubt in my mind. And you know it, too.'

'I *don't* know it. How could I?' George paused, and considered Leonid for a moment before exploding: 'Why did you fucking attack them? What are you, hellbent for death, or what?'

'Calm down, man,' said Phil, who was completely ignored.

'Why did *you* kill them?' replied Leonid rather calmly, vodka in hand. 'You looked to enjoy it a little, I think.'

'You asshole! You gave me no choice! We had to go the whole hog after you flipped the fucking switch!'

'I saved your life in such case. We don't take people in deep wood for to asking questions. We take for make them disappear. Your father was here, he would teach you this.'

George lunged at Leonid, but Phil and Spaska restrained him. 'George, he's right! He has the benefit of experience with these pricks,' Phil said, gently guiding George back into his seat. Leonid was moved by Phil's comment. *Yes, I do have experience.* He impressed himself, and thought hard on the subject. If only he could put that experience into play. He had it, but he couldn't touch it. Not yet.

'Benefit of experience, my ass! Only thing he's got is the benefit of trauma. Didn't you see the way he went off? The look on his face? He's fucked up, Phil!' George turned to face Leonid again. 'You hear me, Leo? You're fucked in the head. Fucked.'

'OK, George. I am fucked in head. And now, you are too. It is truth, no?'

George waved this off and finished his beer.

'We were damn lucky,' Phil said. 'Things would have gone south for us if those guys didn't screw up the way they did.'

'How do you mean?' George's ears pricked up.

'Think about it, guys. We shouldn't have had control of the van. One of their guys should have been at the wheel.'

'That's right,' said Spaska. 'I didn't think of it.'

'Next mistake: we should have gone down the track *before* the APC, not after,' added Phil. 'That way, if something went wrong in our car, they still would have had us blocked in.'

'You're right. We never could have pulled off what we did.' George was beginning to calm down. 'They really did fuck up.'

'And that's why Leo did exactly the right thing. He didn't endanger us. He saved our asses!'

George nodded, averting his gaze from the table, looking skyward, a mess of emotions. Guilt over the murders he had committed that day, side by side with elation. Sadness over his father, coupled with a growing dislike for Leonid. He felt he owed him something, but didn't want to admit that.

'I'm hitting the sack. Gotta think about what I'm gonna tell the embassy people in the morning. Goodnight.'

'And after call, we can leave, yes?' Leonid asked. 'You have seen enough now? We can stop? We still have deal?'

'Yes.'

'Yes? "Yes" for which, George? What, "yes"?'

'Yes, Leonid, yes. Yes, we can leave. Yes, I've had enough. Yes, we still have a deal.' With that, George disappeared into the hostel, drooped in resignation.

'Good. All I want for to hear.'

George grunted as he passed by the body bag in which Conrad was stored, lying on the ground near the threshold – a body bag that had been meant for his father.

BOOK THREE
AMERICA

The decay of the Soviet experiment should come as no surprise to us. Wherever the comparisons have been made between the free and closed societies – West Germany and East Germany, Austria and Czechoslovakia, Malaysia and Vietnam – it is the democratic countries that are prosperous and responsive to the needs of their people. And one of the simple but overwhelming facts of our time is this: of all the millions of refugees we've seen in the modern world, their flight is always away from, not toward the Communist world. Today on the NATO line, our military forces face east to prevent a possible invasion. On the other side of the line, the Soviet forces also face east – to prevent their people from leaving.

President Ronald Reagan
Address to Members of the British Parliament
('The "Evil Empire" Speech')
London, UK, 8 June 1982

NINE

Leonid's first months in Washington, DC were spent living at a level of material comfort he had never known. George had put him up in a two-star bed-and-breakfast in Georgetown; Leonid was to stay there until George had managed to oil the wheels of the immigration process. Leonid's benefactor had promised him that his name would be bumped to the head of the queue, a queue that was 200,000 strong per annum. As much as foreigners might hate the place, they still wanted in. There they might be safe. Maybe.

In the meantime, George gave Leonid a monthly stipend of $2,000 for expenditures such as vodka, Pizza Hut, movies and more vodka. Leonid bought some new clothes as well, but was astonished by the prices. He tried bargaining at a Gap store, and that went nowhere fast; the staff merely laughed at him. It took him a full forty-eight hours to discover the Goodwill and Salvation Army shops in town. He tried bargaining there too, but this time he was met with outright derision.

Life during wartime had effectively cured him of two addictions, drinking and smoking. As soon as he had the opportunity, however, he got straight back to the drinking.

But smoking he had nearly forgotten until his arrival in the States, and when he saw the cost of a pack of smokes, he promptly forgot about that habit again. Oddly, the comparatively high pricing on vodka did not deter him. The vodka was staying put.

Naturally, Leonid had trouble spending the full amount of the stipend, so he began socking large amounts away, as had been his habit back in Moscow. He cut a hole under the box-spring of his bed, storing his cash there. He checked it compulsively, and instructed the staff at the B&B that he and only he would be the one to change the bedsheets in his room.

As for George, keeping his end of the deal had proved wearisome from the beginning. After the whole fiasco in Chechnya, he had felt it prudent not to return to Moscow. The people at the US embassy were not happy with him, nor were certain elements in the Russian government. George mollified his countrymen by arranging for Conrad's body to be flown back to the US on his own dime. He mollified the Russians by simply leaving their country.

They had driven to Tbilisi in Georgia and returned the bullet-ridden van they had rented. Simple payment for damages to the vehicle was not enough to satisfy the Georgian rental company, not once they realized they were dealing with Americans. Large sums were pulled out of George's pockets on that score.

Next, they hopped on an illegal and seriously expensive short plane ride to Ankara, Turkey. Leonid was without any of the sort documents he would need to enter the US. George had to go through a juggernaut of bureaucratic bullshit at the Russian embassy to get him a new passport. Many palms were greased.

Now he was back home, paying for all Leonid's needs. The process of having Leonid naturalized was not going as smoothly as he had hoped. He had carried the Russian along for three months now, and was growing more and more irritated. After all, he never had retrieved his father's body; all that Leonid had provided was his testimony before a Senate committee (comprising mainly Bill Hanson's friends) regarding his captivity in Chechnya. Leonid recounted his experiences in disturbing detail. He had turned out to be quite the storyteller. That testimony gave George part of what he wanted; his father was no longer considered missing. Bill Hanson was now officially dead, and his affairs could be wrapped up. It wasn't exactly closure, but it would suffice.

In the fourth month, Leonid finally received his citizenship, and that having been achieved, George decided it was time to cut him loose. He had fulfilled his obligations, and was frankly sick of looking at Leonid. It never reminded him of anything nice.

Leonid saw things in quite the opposite way. He had imagined that the current arrangement might continue *ad infinitum.* He had delivered the goods; he had saved George's life in Chechnya, told the story of Bill Hanson's murder and was now receiving his deserved reward. He was shocked out of this utopian stupor when George gave him the hard news at a meeting in a Georgetown watering hole.

After ordering drinks up at the bar, George turned Leonid's stool to face him. Without any trace of mirth, he announced: 'Leo, I'm very, very, fully and completely overjoyed to hand this document over to you and to congratulate you on your newfound status as a fucking American.' That said, he plopped a manila envelope containing all the necessary documents down on the bar.

Leonid reached out for the proffered documents, but
George withdrew the envelope and slammed down a shot
of bourbon while signalling for another.

'You know what this means. You *are* one of us now. Got it?'

'Of course I caught it! Now let me to see …'

'Ah, ah, ah. Do you know what else it means?' George
waved the envelope in the air.

'Yes, yes, I am pledging an alliance to a flag …'

'Not that, you moron! No, none of that bullshit! What
it means is: no more allowance for you. No more nothing.
Our deal ends here. You're on your own now, just like
everybody else in this country. And good luck with that!'
George's second bourbon arrived; he made short work of it
and ordered another.

Leonid, wide-eyed, mouth agape, moved his hand on the
surface of the bar in search of his vodka gimlet (a new drink
to which he'd taken a recent liking, but which he only drank
at these meetings when George took care of the tab). He
was having trouble putting his hand to it now. 'No more
payments of the month?'

'No more.' George threw the documents down on the bar.

Leonid found the stem of his glass and slowly lifted it to
his lips. 'No more BB?'

'No more B&B either. You're out at the end of the week.
You should find yourself a place.'

'But I have not work …' Leonid drained the glass and
ordered another.

'Find some, then. You've had months. You've been resting
on your laurels long enough, my friend. You better get busy.'
George shot his third bourbon down and stood to leave.

'But I could not work legal. Not until this day.'

'So work *illegally*. Isn't that what you used to do?'

George made a strong point. Andrei Trofimov's business card was one of the only things Leonid possessed from his life before Chechnya. He had thrown it into a drawer carelessly, and had never bothered to call the man from New York to see about a life in the Mafiya Stateside. He still hadn't even called anyone back in Russia. His dream had come true; he was living in America. He didn't want to think of the past anymore. But he now realized that would prove impossible. His fresh gimlet arrived.

'George, what about drinks?' Leonid said, lifting the glass.

'Looks like they're on you this time, buddy.' George started walking towards the door.

'But this is too expensive on me!'

'Welcome to America, asshole. And by the way, lose my number.' And with that, George was gone.

Leonid put the drink back on the bar, untouched. He stared at it for awhile. *Six dollars for this fucking thing! Maybe I can send it back. How much were George's drinks? How many did he have? Oh God! Om mani padme hum.* (He had taken to repeating the writing on Bill Hanson's ring, the short prayer for peace and compassion, voicing it in his head. It wasn't directed at the wider world, but solely at himself: peace for him, and compassion from others towards him.)

Leonid hailed the bartender.

'Sir? Another cocktail?'

'No! Just bill. And I want for send this one back.'

'Back where, sir?'

'Back! Who is caring where! Back in bottle!'

'Sir, this is a mixed drink. I can't *un-mix* it.'

'Why for not?'

The bartender handed Leonid the bill as he answered the question. 'Because for in this country is not existing the machine for cause of un-mixing of the drinks of cheaplike scumbags.' Leonid didn't even notice the gibe; his eyes went wide at the bill. Money, the acquisition of it, was all that mattered now. Leonid needed a plan, and fast.

He contemplated the vodka gimlet before him. This would be his last. As tight as he was already wearing his belt, he decided that the time for some serious belt-tightening was upon him. He thought back to Moscow, and all the money he had stored in that oven. He thought of the Chechen woods, where he had survived on virtually nothing. Only now that he had everything he wanted did he realize he should have wanted more. Here he was, in the States, the Land of Milk and Honey, Pizza Huts on every other corner – and he could soon be homeless.

He continued to stare down the drink for a while longer and then quaffed it, paid the outrageous bar bill and didn't forget to not tip. *Something in that bartender's tone.*

Then he ran back to the B&B. Ripping the box-spring apart, he began to count what was left of his money.

The time to call Russia had definitely arrived. The question now was, whom should he phone? The list of choices was not long. Miki, the man who had most likely thrown him to the wolves back in Chechnya? Certainly not. His father, a man for whom he had no filial feeling and distrusted absolutely? Of course not. Spaska? He was rotting in a truck on some anonymous street in Grozny. There was only one person alive he could call: his old pizza-gorging, truck-driving buddy, Piotr.

The phone rang interminably. *Probably sleeping one off. Come on, dammit! Pick up!* Yet Leonid had neglected to factor the time difference into the equation. A woman eventually answered. It was Piotr's wife, Natalya, who bellowed into the phone: 'Just tell me quickly! Who died? Tell me, you son of a bitch!'

'It's me, it's Leonid. Calm down. Nobody died, OK?' As he said this, he thought of all the recent dead, the ridiculousness of his comment. *Right. Nobody died! The dead surround us. They are everywhere. They are always.*

'Leonid? Leonid, who? You know what time it is, you asshole!?'

'Natalya, it's me. Leonid Petrovich. I'm calling from America.'

Natalya paused for a moment here before going off her nut. 'Oh my God! You died! You're a ghost! You're already dead!'

Leonid heard her scream, and then the phone dropped. The screaming continued, and then he could make out a man's voice: Piotr. 'Can't you see I'm sleeping here, you crazy bitch! What are you carrying on like a maniac for, did you lose your mind again, or what?'

Piotr then, evidently, walked over to the phone and kicked it across the room. The noise hurt Leonid's ears.

'Yes, woman! It's a fucking phone! And what of it?'

Leonid heard her say: 'It's, it's f-f-for you. May God save us all!' There was another round of screeching, and Leonid heard her footsteps as she ran.

'Crazed witch.' Piotr picked the receiver off the ground and spoke: 'Piotr here. This better be fucking good!'

'Boo! Guess who.' Leonid was laughing now.

'Listen, fuckhead, tell me where you are, come on, just tell me! I'll be there in five minutes to pull your balls off and make you eat them.'

'OK, bigshot, I'm in America. Come and get me.'

'What? America! Who the hell is this?'

'It's Leonid, you idiot. Who did you think it was?'

'Leo? Is that really you …?'

'Yes, of course it's me.'

'But we thought you were dead … I was told …'

'You were told bullshit! It's me, and I'm here, in Washington!'

Piotr was now as stunned as his wife. 'Prove to me it's you. Tell me what only Leonid could know.'

'OK. You ready? The Pizza Huts here are better than the one in Moscow.'

Piotr had to sit down. He now understood that it was indeed Leonid. For so many months he had accepted it as reality that his friend, his enviable friend, was dead and gone. That fact hadn't really upset his life. He could no longer afford to eat in foreign restaurants, but that was about the worst of it. When he first heard the news of Leonid's death he actually smiled to himself while mouthing words of sorrow and loss.

'They've opened a couple of new ones since you left. The queues are getting shorter …' This was all he could muster.

They caught up for another ten minutes before Leonid broached the real subject of his call: accessing the cash in his father's stove, an amount he estimated to be well over $15,000.

'Piotr, I have a favour to ask. A very important favour. But first, I must know that I can trust you.'

'What a fucking insult! Of course you can trust me! And let me ask you, even before you tell me of this famous favour, do you remember your promise to me?'

'What? What are you talking about? What promise?'

'That one night, after we ate at Pizza Hut. Do you remember what you said to me?'

'Don't play games, Piotr. Just tell me the promise.'

'You said that when you finally achieved your big dream of escaping to America, your great big fucking dream, that you would send for me and Natalya and her decrepit old mother. That was your promise to me!'

'I don't recall any such –'

'That's it, big man! Of course you don't remember. I knew you wouldn't!'

'Listen to me, I was probably drunk at the time. Who knows what kinds of promises I made?'

'Excuses! You think I wasn't drunk at the time, too? Still, I remember everything!'

'Calm down, Piotr. A minute ago you thought I was a ghost, now you're screaming at me to bring you over here! It's not so easy! I have to organize things, you understand? Everything here is incredibly expensive, this isn't Russia anymore. Now that's why I'm calling you. If you can help me in this, perhaps it will allow me to keep old promises.'

'Alright, fine. Tell me what you need from me.'

'OK. Now, I never told you this, but I kept a hidden stash of money. You understand?'

The wheels began to turn in Piotr's mind, dreams of hidden treasure he might procure for himself. 'Go on.'

'I need you to get it and send it to me. But this must all be handled with great care.'

'No problem. Just tell me where the money is. And how much, by the way?'

'Never mind that now. It's part of the money I'm going to use to bring you here to America,' Leonid lied. 'That's all you need to know.'

'OK, already! Just tell me where!'

'In my father's flat, in the kitchen, there is a –'

'Oh my God, Leonid!'

'What? What now?'

'I forgot to tell you …'

'Tell me what?'

'About your father …'

'Yes, what about him?'

'He's dead.'

'Dead? How is he dead?'

'In the fire!'

Leonid's face whitened. He remembered his vision in Grozny. 'What fucking fire?'

'In the flat. He burned down the whole building, along with himself!'

Leonid was sweating. He didn't say anything in response.

'After you died he was alone and –'

'I never died, Piotr, you damn fool!'

'I'm sorry … when he heard of your death … he had to start doing things by himself. They say he was trying to cook. That the stove was the origin of the fire. The building went up like a box of matches. Luckily his screaming alerted the others. They all escaped with their lives. But your father, he was burnt to a crisp.'

'*Now* you're telling me this!' *Om mani padme hum.*

'What can I say, I was shocked to hear from you. Besides, I know there was no love lost between you and your father.'

Piotr was right. After he had a moment to sort things through, Leonid felt it was worth every penny of his currency to hear of the old man's accidental immolation, to finally acquire the status of 'orphan' that he had longed for.

'Leonid, are you still there?'

'Yes, I'm here.'

'You were about to tell me where the money was.'

Leonid pulled the business card from his breast pocket and wordlessly disconnected the line. Yet again, things had changed up on him. He dialled a new number, the New York number of Andrei Lvovich Trofimov.

Back in Moscow, Piotr broke his phone into pieces and stormed into the kitchen for some hard vodka drinking, his brain screaming about lost and sunken treasure. Natalya was trembling next to the toilet, having run there and locked herself in when confronted with a ghost from the past; Piotr neglected to relieve her from this posting.

❉

'Mr Trofimov's office. Who may I say is calling?'

Leonid was very impressed. *He has a secretary! That's class. Even Miki didn't have one. The bartender took his calls. What a scumbag.* 'Here is Leonid Petrovich Koshkin talking. Is possible speak with Andrei?'

'One moment, sir, I'll see if he's available.' A moment later, Andrei was on the line. He spoke in Russian.

'Leonid, how are you, my old friend?'

'You remember me?'

'Of course. In business, it is very important to remember people and names. I must tell you, I'm surprised to hear from you.'

'Why is that?'

'Before I left Moscow last winter, I was led to believe that you had met with an accident in Chechnya.'

'Miki told you it was an accident?'

'To be frank, he told me that you had died.' Leonid was very curious to know exactly what kind of stories Miki had been telling. Piotr's information had been useless, of course; Piotr was an outsider. He was not Mafiya.

'And exactly how did I "die", if you don't mind?'

'I'm sorry to tell you this, but he said you had been driving drunk, and collided with an oncoming truck. He was actually very upset with you.'

That motherfucking dog. Om mani padme hum! 'It seems that Miki was mistaken, wouldn't you say. Maybe he was drunk when he told you that story.' Leonid chuckled, but was boiling with rage. Of course, he would not reveal this to someone as proper as Andrei.

'Ha, ha, yes, perhaps. So tell me, where are you now, my reincarnated friend?'

'I'm here in America. In DC.'

'That's incredible. Are you enjoying it?'

'Very much, yes.'

'Are you here on work?'

'Actually, that's why I'm calling. I'm looking for work.'

'So you're here to stay, then?'

'Yes, I have full citizenship.'

'Impressive. And Miki doesn't know your whereabouts?'

'Like you said, he thinks I'm dead.'

'It's not wise to talk business over the phone, but are you still *in*?' Leonid grasped the implication.

'You tell me, Andrei Lvovich.'

'I see. It's a delicate question. Let me make some calls. How can I reach you?'

'I'm in the process of moving. I'll have to call you back when I have a private phone.'

'Alright, then. Call my office back in one week, and we'll see where we're at then.'

Leonid thanked him and hung up. What was his status now that Miki had sent him out to create an ambush? He had no idea. The story of his survival was now most certainly going to reach Miki's ears. How would he react? Leonid had an attack of acute paranoia: Miki might try and have him killed. Why not? After all, he'd tried it before. After all the shit he'd been through, he was going to get whacked in America. *That phone call was a big fucking mistake! I'm dead!*

Leonid went to the nearest bar and started throwing them back until he calmed himself down. *They don't know where I am. I don't even have a place yet. Besides, I'm a small fish, why should they come hunting me? These are busy people.* He paid his tab and headed back to the B&B. *Wheel of Fortune* would be coming on the television shortly. He'd grown rather fond of the show over these last few months.

'How much?!' Leonid gaped at the woman showing him the small and dingy two-room flat.

'For the last time, it's $1,500 a month. That doesn't include electricity or heating.'

'You are sure of this?'

'Yes!'

'For shithole, you want me for to spend fifteen hundred? Maybe in *roubles* …'

'No. Dollars. American dollars.'

'Could rent castle for less. I have idea you are playing joke with me.'

'Look, you want it or not? I have others waiting to see it today.'

'I am paying you two hundred and fifty. No more!'

'Alright, Boris, that does it! Let's go. Time for you to leave.' She grabbed his arm and led him to the door, locked it behind her and started down the stairs.

Leonid was still on the landing, watching her descend. 'We have deal, yes?'

She did not reply.

It was difficult to get a handle on real estate in this new land, and Leonid was still searching for a place in posh Georgetown. With nearly $7,500 to his name that he had managed to save, he felt himself a rich man – but he was certainly not rich enough to handle the prices of the neighbourhood. After looking at four apartments in one afternoon, he was beginning to understand this.

He had one more place to check out that day. It was not in Georgetown. Rather than splurge on the five-dollar cab ride, he opted for the bus. It was on this bus that he had a revelation: across from him, he saw the ever-familiar Pizza Hut logo sewn onto the breast pocket of a shirt worn by an elderly black man.

Leonid was still growing accustomed to DC's large African–American population. There were Africans in Moscow, but he'd had virtually no interaction with them; he'd mostly known black people from films and television, and had a vague notion that they were oppressed by the white capitalist system. The Party had pushed it down people's throats back home for years, but until he'd come to America, he'd figured that had all just been bullshit propaganda, like everything else it had put out.

Leonid felt an immediate connection. Was he not oppressed himself? By what or by whom he could scarcely express – the list in his head was far too long for that. Still, were he and this black man not brothers in oppression? Of course they were! Leonid moved from his own seat and took the empty one beside the man.

'Excuse me, but may I ask where you are living?' Leonid fixed the man with this question directly, yet politely. The man believed at first that Leonid had been addressing someone else, but then felt Leonid's eyes on him in expectation of a reply. He gave Leonid a long once-over, then, generously, decided the Russian was just a harmless and eccentric tourist rather than some nutjob.

'Where are you from, son?'

'Am coming from Russia.'

'Russia, huh? So why do you want to know where I live?'

'Am looking for accommodations,' Leonid replied.

'With *me*?!'

'No, no! But in area of your accommodations. Pizza Hut logo is sign of highest quality. Will lead for good housing.'

The elderly man looked down at the logo on his shirt, then up again at Leonid, and raised his eyebrows. He thought about reassessing his appraisal of Leonid's sanity or lack thereof. 'You're looking for a house in my area? Well now, I wouldn't advise that.'

'Why for not?'

'Let's just put it this way: where I live, they don't see a whole lot of white folks.'

'Is OK. Can you take me?'

The man thought on it for a few moments before answering. He cocked his head to one side. 'I'll make you a deal. I'll take you in and show you around for a while on two conditions. One, you promise to stay by my side. Two, you leave before dark. Deal?'

'Yes, deal.'

The two men shook hands on it.

'I'm Fred. What do I call you?'

Leonid told Fred his name and then asked for the name of the borough. After Fred pronounced it, Leonid was in love. He had never heard such a beautiful name. He was already dreaming of living there. 'Is available for to rent any inexpensive accommodations there?'

'Ain't nothing but!' laughed Fred.

Thus Leonid decided to skip his other appointment and follow Fred home to a place across the river called Anacostia.

TEN

Within a few days, Leonid was comfortably ensconced in his first real home since becoming an orphan. He had moved to Anacostia, and was fully embracing his new neighbourhood. There was a Pizza Hut just a few blocks away up near the river, which he frequented. Liquor stores were abundant. He had bought himself a nice television set that, he was quite sure, was non-exploding. Other than that, he didn't need much. He kept his place minimalist in style: bed, chair, table, fridge and the TV. The flat had come with a stove as well, which on occasion he would eye suspiciously but never use.

Of course, he viewed Anacostia from quite a different perspective than the average white resident of his newly adopted city. Sure, there was occasional sporadic gunfire, and yes, the strong police presence did sometimes feel more like a military occupation than anything else. True, it had a higher murder rate than any other neighbourhood in DC, a city rife with bad neighbourhoods and the murder capital of the US. Then, of course, there were the stares he got for being one of the few white people living in a predominantly black and occasionally brown community.

All that was nothing to Leonid. By this point, he'd lived through so much worse than Anacostia; it was, comparatively speaking, Paradise. He had but one complaint: the plumbing in his building. He had suffered bad plumbing his whole life, and felt this should not be an issue in his adopted country. On the first day after moving in, he had begun to hound the building's superintendent, which he would continue to do on a daily basis.

'This can not be in America!' he would shout while poking a finger into the super's chest. The neighbours stuck their heads into the hallway to see what all the commotion was about. 'Toilet must flush shit out! Not for pull more in! Fix it! Fix it! Fix it!'

The super was a stubborn old curmudgeon, and simply waved off Leonid with a 'Bah!', taking him for a lunatic. Every day Leonid would accost him and start yelling, and every day the super would walk away, ignoring him. But by the fifth day, support for Leonid's cause had swelled amongst the tenants. Now when they stuck their heads out, it wasn't just to watch the one-act play. They were becoming part of the show. After all, was Leonid's cause not their own?

'He's right, man! We're sick of this here shit! And I do mean literal!'

'Why don't you drag them old bones to the basement and fix the damn thing?'

'You don't take care of this soon, someone gonna do you up right!'

Their support heartened Leonid. He felt like the leader in an epic battle for an efficacious system of sanitation. 'You see, everyone agrees. Now you fix!' Leonid poked the super again, always in the exact same spot.

The super, however, remained unmoved. 'Fuck all y'all! We've been living this way for as long as anyone can remember, and that's the way we're gonna die. Anyway, you can kiss my damn bony ass because there ain't no money to fix this plumbing!'

'No! You kiss our assholes, headshit!' Leonid shouted back, indicating the growing crowd with the sweeping gesture of one hand while poking the super with a finger from the other. 'How much for to fix? Tell me!'

'Why? What are you gonna do, huh? You gonna foot the bill now, is that it?'

Leonid was far too thrifty with his money to go all in by himself on the challenge, but he didn't want to lose face. He addressed himself to the other tenants: 'Fellow people who are living in occupied space here under common roof, please come for to drink vodka and discuss problem of shit at seven-thirty in this evening, direct after *Wheel of Fortune*. We will plan solution together as one!'

The crowd applauded. They approved. The older women amongst them were especially impressed by the foreigner's apparent respect for their viewing habits. The superintendent was not amused.

'What the fuck is this! Why you listenin' to this commie for? What the hell is this white boy doin' here anyhow? Huh? You come in here to organize some kind of damn union or something? I'm tellin' y'all right now, the owner is *not* gonna be too keen on no goddamn tenants' meeting. He might even start handing out eviction notices once he gets wind of this! You can believe that!'

Leonid's fellow tenants were incensed.

'Fuck that slumlord! We ain't even ever seen him around these parts, the chickenshit!'

'Let him come down here and try and evict my ass!'

'Come on, everybody, let's get organized!' one man said. 'Who's gonna show tonight at' – here he faltered – 'what's your name?'

'Name is Leonid, Apartment 4F.'

'Cool. They call me Quince.' The man came over to Leonid and the two of them shook hands. Quince addressed the crowd again: 'So who's coming to Leonid's tonight? Let's see some hands!'

It was agreed; everyone would be there.

'Tell all your neighbours to come on up to Leonid's tonight too,' added Quince. 'Number 4F!'

Leonid was definitely going to need more vodka.

❁

Leonid and Fred had become fast friends after their meeting on the bus, and of course it had been Fred who had hooked Leonid up with his new flat. He'd tried to dissuade him from moving to the area, but Leonid could not be convinced, and after much protesting, Fred gave in and helped him sort some minor details. Without acknowledging the fact to Leonid, Fred had decided to look out for him, make sure no one fucked around with him too much.

They met regularly down at the corner bar for a short drink after Fred finished his shift at the Pizza Hut across the Moat – for that's what many Anacostia residents called the river that divided them from their President, their government and the rest of their country. 'The Moat': no one could tell you anymore who had originated the expression, what great wit, but it was believed to be over a hundred years old – probably more. On one side of the Moat lay the castle. On the other side lay the hinterland of the American South.

Leonid was already hitting the vodka when Fred walked in. A shot of bourbon awaited the older man. Fred walked over and grabbed the stool next to Leonid's.

'How's it going, buddy.' Fred sipped his drink and patted Leonid's back by way of thanks.

'Same thing always. Toilet trouble. I am looking for your advices, my friend.'

'Like I've been telling you, the owner's never going to pay for that stuff. Hell, why do you think you got such a cheap rent? It's like they say: you get what you pay for.'

'No, not for this instance! Things are changing today. All of building has agreed to meet for talk this night. We will fight against owner.'

Fred ordered another round for them both and listened carefully as Leonid recounted the events of the day. He had to pay close attention because, truthfully, Leonid's eccentric syntax exasperated him.

Leonid wanted a second opinion regarding his plan. He told Fred that if all the people living in his building could contribute a certain amount towards the repairs to the plumbing, he was prepared to make up the difference. It was that important to him.

'But where're you going find that kind of money, Leo? You ain't even working yet! These are poor folk, too, son. They can't be coming up with a whole hell of a lot. Now, I don't know about Russia, but plumbers over here get rich, and but quick!'

'I have some money in mattress.'

Fred laughed.

'Seriously? You're too much!'

Leonid had begun to notice a change in the way people interacted with him. Back in Russia, no one ever laughed at his comments; they were taken as cold, hard facts. But since he had been around Americans, everybody was laughing, as though his comments were something other than fact – as if they were meant to sound ironic.

Fred chuckled again before getting down to business. 'Listen up, now. If you all, you and everyone else in the tenement, can come up with half the cost, the owner might kick in the rest. Don't go offering him up the whole deal. Got to negotiate, play it out. You hear?'

Leonid did hear. He rather liked Fred's idea of saving himself some money. In fact, he loved it.

The week that Leonid and Andrei had agreed upon had passed – and just in time, too. Leonid needed to know his next move. This plumbing thing was presenting him with several problems. As he dialled the number, he felt a chill. The paranoia was coming back. Maybe this was a bad idea.

Andrei's secretary answered and patched Leonid through immediately. Andrei was ebullient. 'Leonid! You have excellent timing, my friend!'

'How are you, Andrei? You sound very happy.'

'Of course I'm happy. Why should it be otherwise, when I have good news to deliver!'

Oh my God. This is it – I'm dead. Om mani padme hum. 'What good news?'

'You were a driver, correct? You know your way around an engine?'

'That was my training, yes.'

'Well, my friend, it turns out that the esteemed Anton Sarkhov has need of your services.'

Leonid recognized the name. Sarkhov was a known scammer who had managed to swindle American oil companies out of countless millions of dollars back in the Seventies. The Communists had become fed up with his grift of their graft. They yanked him out of prison in 1968, labelling him a 'refusenik' and thus enabling Sarkhov – as well as other criminals the Party saw off in similar fashion – to emigrate. These undesirables slipped in alongside the Jews, dissidents and other genuine refuseniks granted permission to exit. Sarkhov was famous in all the wrong circles.

'Does that mean I'm still *in*?'

'Yes, Leonid, it does. And you need not worry about Miki, either.'

Leonid remarked to himself on Andrei's insight into his own fears. Clearly, there was a possibility that Miki resented his survival; but Andrei's remark assuaged Leonid's nerves. He was in America, and he was clear.

'There is a problem,' Leonid said. 'As you may know, I lost all my documents in Chechnya. That means I have no driver's permit.'

'But you have your passport, yes?'

'Yes.'

'Then everything will be arranged. Your permit will be replaced.'

Leonid felt relief wash over him. 'Thank you, Andrei Lvovich. How can I ever repay you ...?'

'There's no need for that. Just do the job well.'

'Of course. What is the job, exactly?'

'Personal driver to Mr Sarkhov. He lives in DC now, so it's right in your neighbourhood. Let me ask, how well do you know the town?'

'I know certain parts very well.'

'You must study the map, then. He will be moving around a lot.'

'Will the maps be correct? Maybe I should walk around, find out what's what.'

'This isn't Russia, my friend; the maps here are correct.'

'I see.' *That's what they all say.* 'May I ask what became of his former driver?'

'I'm afraid he died.'

'Died?'

'It was an unfortunate incident.'

Leonid was back to feeling anxious. Did he really want to dance with the Devil again? 'I'll study the maps well.' *Om mani padme hum.*

'Good. And Leonid, I'm sure I don't have to say this, but … no drinking. Understood?'

'Yes. Of course.' And Leonid *did* understand. This was not Russia. You couldn't just drive around in an altered state all the time without any consequences. And this certainly wasn't Chechnya, where it only made good goddamn sense to drive around drunk as a bastard, especially if you were dumb enough to go there in the first place. This was America. Here you would meet with fines and possible jail terms for such behaviour. It wasn't that these people weren't drinking and driving all over the place. He knew this from the nightly news, *COPS* and Teddy Kennedy. It was just that Americans of all stripes, from top to bottom, were paying those fines and doing those jail terms.

❁

The day after hosting the tenants in his flat, Leonid was back at it again, poking the super in the chest and making demands in front of a crowd. It had been agreed that all the tenants would pay towards the repairs, each according to his or her means, and Leonid would take care of the rest. But first they needed an idea of just how much this would cost.

'How much for fix?' Leonid thundered. 'Give me total price!'

At this point, the super was wincing from the jabs. He had developed a bruise from Leonid's constant poking, and it was growing larger with each thrust. The old man knew it would never have the chance to heal if Leonid didn't relent – and he was beginning to understand that Leonid never would.

'Alright! Alright! I'll tell you! But first get that fucking finger off my titty! It'll be in the neighbourhood of seven grand. What do you have to say to that, huh?! You got that kind of money?' The super then addressed the crowd: 'Does any of you broke-ass niggers have that kind of cash?!'

Leonid was a bit shocked to hear that figure, but he stuck to his guns. He was quite sure – although perhaps a bit prematurely – that this new job would work out. 'Tell the boss we will pay the half for!' The other tenants started clapping their hands together and cheering.

'Fine, motherfucker! I'll tell him. But he ain't gonna like it!' The super turned his back on the assembly, and stormed off.

Leonid called out after him: 'And my mother, she dead in ground – but your mother, your mother we can talk of!' At that, the other tenants roared with laughter.

Everyone in the corridor shook hands and congratulated themselves, but really, it was Leonid's day. Within a week, the plumbing situation was righted. The owner of the building couldn't believe his luck; complaints to the rental board had been piling up, and he was expecting to be forced to fix the problem and pay several stiff fines for code violations at any moment. Leonid's rash actions had saved the slumlord thousands. The tenants pulled just over a thousand dollars from their own pockets, and Leonid, as promised, paid the difference. Nobody really understood what a sham the whole affair had been, except those who possessed the right information. As usual, Leonid was amongst those who did not.

Nevertheless, Leonid was now firmly established as a hero, and a legend in the community. Walking down the street, he might overhear some complete stranger who would nudge their friend and exclaim: 'There he is, that's the Toilet Guy!' It became his new moniker and he was proud of it, wore it like a badge. The *faux* hero of the Shitty Toilet Wars.

❂

Andrei had given Leonid very specific instructions as to what this new driver job would entail, and how he was to go about it. First, he needed to go out and buy himself a black suit – several, in fact, along with a dozen white shirts and black ties. Appearance was of the utmost importance, he explained, for Sarkhov would be meeting with people at the highest echelons of society, types who did not even realize they were dealing with a criminal.

Leonid remembered some films he had seen with chauffeurs. 'Should I buy a cap, too?' he asked.

'No. But sunglasses are a must. He will want you to appear to be a member of the Secret Service.'

Leonid's first day on the job would require much discretion. He was to arrive promptly at a certain parking garage, dressed as instructed, head to Level B, Section 8 and locate a black Cadillac.

'And then?'

'Then, you will wait. Everything will be explained. And Leonid, upon your first meeting with Mr Sarkhov, you will say nothing. He will give you a destination, and you will drive him to it. Do not attempt any chit-chat. Mr Sarkhov is a man of few words. You should consider yourself as a mute.'

'In short, I shut up and drive.'

'How well you put it.'

Leonid bought the black suits, white shirts, black ties and sunglasses. Wearing them made him feel odd, as though he belonged to some kind of organization or worse, a cult. Although he was actually working for a crime organization, this was not what one wore. Not back in Russia. Most of the guys back there looked as if they were going to a gymnasium; the fatter ones, always sweating, looked as if they were coming back from one.

Leonid found the parking garage and went to Level B, Section 8. He arrived promptly at 9.00 AM and located the Cadillac easily. Two men stood beside it, dressed in exactly the same fashion as Leonid. He approached them.

'I am the new driver,' he said in Russian.

'Very good. Let me explain the rules to you,' said one of the anonymous men. He did not introduce himself. The other one held back, just stood there looking, thought Leonid, like a douchebag. A douchebag in the mirror.

'The rules?'

'The car stays here. Always. Unless you are driving Mr Sarkhov. The car must be picked up here, and it must be returned here at the end of your shift.'

'So you're not Sarkhov, then?'

'Of course not.'

'Where is he?'

'He is where he is.'

'OK, so give me the keys and the address and I'll go pick him up.'

The man turned to his partner. 'Can you believe this guy?' Then he pulled out a Glock 9 and repeated: 'The car stays here. It's not for your personal use. You understand?'

Om mani padme hum! 'OK, OK! I understand. I'm not a car thief. I never even owned one. I'm just the driver.'

The man turned the gun around and handed it to Leonid. 'Take it. Carry it with you. Always.'

Leonid accepted the gun with trepidation. 'Why do I need this?'

The man opened the door on the driver's side and handed Leonid the keys. 'It's insurance. Now get in.'

'Where am I going?'

The man gave him an address near Dupont Circle, and ushered him into the car. Leonid had studied well, and now knew all the streets and parts of town. He also knew their reputations.

'The gay part of town?'

'Watch your mouth. Never speak of this. Now get going. Mr Sarkhov is waiting, and you should never keep him waiting.' With that, he slammed the door shut and walked away with his partner.

❋

At the appointed time, Leonid pulled the specially bullet-proofed car up to a sleazy address, a sauna flying a multicoloured flag that he couldn't place. Punctually, a large, dapper man in his sixties with a regal air descended the stairs. Leonid got out of the car and opened the back door for Mr Sarkhov. Although no one had told him to do so, he understood that he must. Such was the stature of this man.

Sarkhov barely acknowledged him, and sat himself down in the back seat. After Leonid got back into the vehicle, Sarkhov gave him an address – that of the embassy of the Russian Federation on Wisconsin Avenue, near the Naval Observatory.

❖

Leonid's return to Anacostia after his first day at work raised many eyebrows out in the street. He was, after all, spiffed up in a way the residents had never seen him before – all in black, like he was indeed in the Secret Service. He looked, as Quince remarked, like 'hot shit on ice!'.

The questions started in right away as a small crowd formed around him. Was he working for the Man? If so, were they gonna have problems with him? How much cake did he make? Are we gonna have a block party to celebrate? He wasn't moving back across the Moat, was he? Did a piece come with the suit? And once again, was he working for the Man, or what?

Leonid answered to the best of his ability: 'Yes, I work for man. Many men.'

'No, man!' Quince attempted to break the language barrier. Not "men" – "man"! *The* Man.'

'What is name of this man?'

'The Man is the System, Leonid! Like the police. Do you work for the cops?'

'Ah, I see now. You are being funny. Of course I am not working with police.'

'Cool. So who *are* you working with?'

Naturally, Leonid hadn't brought up his past with the Mafiya, even though he knew it could buy him 'street cred'. He decided to stick with that policy, and told his acquaintances simply that he worked in an office. The pay was shit, he would add, and he was not moving anywhere. And, he lied, of course he didn't have a gun. Actually, the Glock made him feel uncomfortable, so he'd left it in the glove compartment of the Cadillac. He was only required to carry it while working, after all.

The last lie pricked up Oz's ears. Oz was the local gun wrangler. He knew of Leonid, as did most people round the neighbourhood, and had shared drinks with him by the corner store. As the crowd dispersed, he came forward and put an arm around Leonid's shoulders. 'You can't afford to be walkin' around these parts, dressed like that, with no piece! Am I right, Quince?'

Quince agreed. It was one thing when Leonid had been dressed like a slob, but now that he'd classed himself up a bit, it was a different story.

'I'm not sayin' you need to worry about *us* – we all cool. We like you.' It was true, too. Leonid had been on the inside since taking care of the plumbing problem.

Oz began to walk Leonid towards a nearby alley as he continued to hold forth. Quince and a few of his buddies followed behind them.

'Nah, it's not us you need to worry about. But let's say you stray a couple of streets east, or a couple of streets west or – and God help you if you do – a couple of streets *south*, dressed in these threads, somebody is goin' to take an interest!' He stopped at the alley.

'Now just wait here a quick second and we'll see what we can hook you up with.'

As Oz disappeared into the alley, Leonid thought about his advice. He still couldn't fathom why these Americans had such an obsession with guns. It seemed that just about everyone in the neighbourhood had one, and these were some of the friendliest people he'd ever known. In Moscow, he could understand the need for guns. Everyone was suspicious and covetous of everyone else. You could be killed over a loaf of bread. But in Moscow, no one had the money for a gun. Yet here was a community where people talked in the street, helped each other out, shared everything – and yet they were fixated on firearms! It made no sense. And while Leonid might actually need a gun in his new line of work, he had one already. *That* was where the danger lay for him, not on fucking Martin Luther King, Jr Avenue.

Nevertheless, Oz returned and presented Leonid with a snub-nosed .38 revolver. Leonid took it in one hand.

'So what do you think? Ain't much, but it'll do the job.'

'Not so bad,' Leonid replied. He fiddled around with the gun, pointing it all over the place. Quince and his buddies moved away from the barrel each time.

'Careful with that!' Oz said. 'It's loaded. You know how to use a gun, right?'

'Of course, am Russian. I know how for to use gun since boy!'

With that, he blew out the passenger window of a parked Delta 88. 'Shit, man, I told you, be careful!' Oz grabbed the gun from Leonid's hand.

A middle-aged man came running out of the corner store upon hearing the shot. In fact, he came running because of the sound of shattering glass; a gunshot in and of itself hardly registered anymore. He was worried it might be his car that had taken the hit. He was right, too.

'What the fuck, motherfuckers!'

'Nothing the fuck,' Leonid retorted.

'What?'

'You ask what the fuck, and I give answer. Gun shoot car window ... is accident.'

'The *gun* did, now, did it!' The man turned on Oz: 'Well, what are you going to do about this?'

'Whoa, wasn't me, man! I was just trying to show my boy here how to use the thing. What he said: it was like an accident.'

'Well one of *you* is going to pay for that goddamn window glass, that's for damn sure!'

Leonid pulled out his bankroll. 'OK, OK, I am paying damage. How much dollars?'

The man peered at the wad, along with everyone else in the little group. 'Eh, well let's see, now ... the car is a classic, of course, so, uh ... let's call it three hundred even, and everyone just walks away.'

Leonid slipped three C-notes into the man's hand, and felt everyone's eyes on him. 'OK now, Oz, how much I pay for gun?'

'Uh ... the gun ain't no thing, two hundred ought to do the trick.'

Leonid peeled off two more bills and handed them to Oz.

'Yo, Leo, what about that block party?' asked Quince, sensing his friend might be on a roll. 'Next Friday, maybe?'

'OK. Fine. Block party. On Friday. Excuse me now, is time for *Wheel of Fortune.*'

Oz and Quince bid Leonid farewell and congrats on the new job. Then they moved over to the corner store and started making plans for the big party.

ELEVEN

One evening, as Leonid and Fred enjoyed their ritual post-work meeting at the local bar, Quince showed up to run the plans for the upcoming block party by Leonid. The three of them sat in a booth. Quince moved on to the cost breakdown: 'Now, the DJ and all his gear would have cost you seven hundred dollars for the night, but when I told him who you were and all you done for the 'hood, he agreed to do it for five bills.'

'Only for five *Amerikanski* dollars?'

'No, man! Five *hundred Amerikanskis*, as you call 'em. I like that. Think I might start using that line. That is, if you don't mind, Leo.'

'Is gift, from Russia to you.'

'Cool beans. Now, it being a party in your honour, you ought to pay out for some drinks. I reckon about two hundred forties. Now, I know it sounds like a lot, but I got you a great deal with Jimmy down at the corner store. He's gonna let you prepay those at two-thirds of the cost. He knows this shit's gonna be big, and once these people get started up drinking and dancing, they won't be stoppin' anytime soon. He stand to get rich off of this here!'

Leonid just nodded. This party was going to cost him more than he had ever spent on any single thing in his life, at least since the toilets in the building. But what the hell. This was his new country; his dream had come true, and it should be celebrated. This was his own personal Fourth of July.

'Next, my boy Skelly is gonna take care of the food. He'll be chargin' folks like at a restaurant, so he'll be makin' his own cake. You don't need to worry on that.'

'What kind of fool name is that?' exclaimed Fred. 'Skelly!'

'It's a Jamaican name, man.'

'Does that mean we're going be getting some jerk cooking at this shindig?'

'Most certainly, my brother.'

'Well, then, that's alright with me. Damn, I do love that stuff!'

Fred laughed, and Quince laughed back: 'Who don't!'

Leonid watched the two men slap hands, wondering if they were calling someone a jerk or if it was some kind of expression. He didn't let it bother him.

'So that is all for time being?'

'Yeah. Excepting one thing, but that's gonna be a surprise for you at the end of the night.'

'I am not liking surprises. Tell it now.'

Fred rubbed Leonid's shoulder reassuringly and winked at him. 'Don't worry, Leo, it's a damn good surprise.'

Quince concurred, and, wearing a sly grin, added: 'Might even be more than one.' He laughed again before quieting down, not wanting to show his hand. Fred chuckled, and Leonid changed the subject.

'Fred, I have question on Pizza Hut. You are expert on this subject, yes?'

Fred laughed once again. 'Yes, I suppose I am. What do you need?'

'This one here in Anacostia, by bridge, never want for deliver me pizza.'

Quince jumped on that one: 'Hell, no! 'Course not. That shit only gets delivered across the Moat. They don't want their drivers getting all shot up over here in Anacostia. You want a pie from them, you best go down and fetch it!'

'Quince is right on the money there. That pie is for the white man up on Capitol Hill. Hell, that pie is even going up to the White House, I bet.'

'Clinton is eating of the pizza you are telling?' Leonid asked.

Fred laughed. 'What *ain't* that boy eating!'

Quince chuckled at that, too. 'Yo, man, what you need that shit for anyway? Pizza Hut serves up the worst pie 'round here! You need to get some local stuff, place called Pendeli's, down in yourself.'

'Is better than at Hut?'

'Hell, yes! The Hut ain't but a chain store. That pie is comin' off the *factory line*. My boy at Pendeli's, he's a brother, you understand, but he worked at some old-timey Italian place back in the day. Those old ginos showed him the ropes, how to do a pie up right. He's carryin' on the tradition right over here now. And he'll get it delivered right up to your front door.'

Fred agreed: 'That is some tasty pie, that Pendeli's.'

'But Fred, you are even employee of Hut! How can you say such thing?'

'Because it's the truth, my friend.'

Leonid could not believe his ears. Quince wrote down a phone number for him and slid it across the table. 'Do yourself a favour, my man, and dial those digits up tonight! You'll never look at the Hut again.'

Leonid did as told and never looked back. Indeed, Pendeli's was the best pizza he had ever tasted.

❁

One full week of driving Sarkhov around town, and the man had still said barely a word to Leonid. Every day was the same. Leonid would pick up the Cadillac at the garage and meet Sarkhov at the gay sauna in Dupont Circle at 9.30 on the dot. He remembered the Frenchman Miki had had beaten up, and what he had said against the Mafiya on television. *Maybe there are a lot of homosexuals in the Mafiya. Who knows? As long as they keep their hands to themselves, why should I care?*

The first stop of the day was usually the Russian embassy. Leonid would wait outside for Sarkhov for at least two hours, and then they would eat. Sarkhov always had a different lunch date; Leonid would eat in the car. Lunch would take nearly two hours as well. Leonid noticed immediately that Sarkhov would take several drinks with all his meals. Once he was sure that this was the man's habit, and despite Andrei's orders against so doing, Leonid began drinking at lunch, too. He brought several small airplane bottles of vodka with him each day, vodka being nearly odourless and generally detectable only by a completely sober person. The rest of the day was spent driving from one of Sarkhov's businesses to another, until Sarkhov was satisfied that everything was in order. Leonid was never told anything of the businesses, and was glad not to know. Leonid would then drop Sarkhov off at his luxury apartment on K Street and return the Cadillac to the parking garage. It was a simple enough job.

He was a glorified cab driver, and that was fine with him. It paid extremely well, and for all Leonid's worries at the beginning, it seemed as safe as could be.

On one occasion Sarkhov had Leonid stop in a commercial area teeming with workers of South Asian origin. Leonid waited patiently in the car, watching the hustle and bustle of people at work, many of them seemingly in the lucrative industry of knock-off brands – probably why Sarkhov was down there to begin with. As he sucked down an airplane bottle's worth of vodka, it occurred to him that perhaps someone in this neighbourhood knew something about the kind of ring Bill Hanson had purchased in India, and could perhaps tell him where he could procure the *om mani padme hum* band right here in town. The fingers of his right hand still subconsciously wandered over to the finger of his left in search of it, always to be left wanting for whatever solace it could offer, even after all this time had passed, since he had returned it to George. He got out of the car and stopped a man pushing a huge cart of textiles. '*Om mani padme hum*,' he repeated over and over, motioning to his ring finger. The man nearly rolled the load over him in annoyance, shouting that worst of all Hindi insults behind him: '*Madarchod!*'

Leonid returned it back to the man in English: 'You are motherfucker here! Not me.' (Somehow, he'd understood. Languages are funny that way; you never know when you're going to pick up some bits and pieces of a new one.)

Leonid didn't have time for this. Sarkhov would be back anytime now. He decided to leave the underlings to their business and find the fat cats. Looking around, he spotted an Indian restaurant that seemed a little too pricey: the kind of place in which management might take their lunch. As he entered the establishment, he came upon several well-dressed Indian men settling their bills. He decided to use his driver's uniform to his advantage. 'Excuse me gentlemens for to disturb,' he addressed them. They all turned to face him. 'I am of the Secret Servicing. I am needing information on you men's culture for relating to criminal atrocities in this area.' Leonid made sure his Glock was visible in its shoulder holster. The Indian men looked as though they might lose their lunches. One of them spoke up: 'What information is it you are needing?'

'I am in search of man with special ring. The ring say on it, with Sanskrit, four little words: *Om mani padme hum.* You know of this expression, yes?'

'Yes …'

'I need you for tell me where I can find such type of ring.'

The men spoke amongst themselves in Hindi. Finally, one of them surrendered a business card and told Leonid: 'It is a shop selling Indian merchandise, my good sir. My no-good brother in-law is the proprietor. I can assure you, I have no dealings with him. None at all!'

Leonid left them wordlessly, and ran back to the Cadillac just as Sarkhov was coming out of a building. He opened the rear passenger door for him and drove away, leaving the Indian men in a state of complete bewilderment. Who could tell what kind of domino effect his actions might have? Someone might catch a beating or worse over this. *Om mani padme hum* be damned, he wanted that fucking ring!

A few days later he had it, too. He found the shop and bought an even more attractive one than Hanson's. No brass for him, with its greening effect upon the skin. No, he bought his ring in silver, a purer metal. The shop carried the ring in gold as well, but Leonid was too cheap to buy that one. He wanted purity, not saintliness.

✹

'Play some Motown, boy! You ever heard of Motown? Hell, you still wet behind the ears!' a woman in her late forties admonished the DJ, egged on by her husband across the way. The husbands, still lovingly seeing their wives as hot young things, would send them over to influence the DJ. Fred was there too, amongst the older generation, urging his wife to get their own song played so they could get some dancing in.

The DJ had heard it all before, and knew the older folks' tastes from previous block parties in the neighbourhood.

'It's comin' up, it's comin'. I gotta serve everyone here, you know. Now just tell me what you want to hear tonight, beautiful. A little Supremes? Some Temptations? Say some Marvin, maybe, or even Smokey?' He laughed. 'Anything you want, sugar.'

The woman softened like butter in a microwave. 'Could you play *These Arms of Mine?*'

'You know I can and will, baby. But that's Otis, and he ain't of Motown.'

She went cold and hard again: 'I know that, motherfucker! Just play the shit!'

The block party was held in front of the corner store. The DJ was set up on the porch on one side, and on the other the owners were doling out cold forty-ouncers of beer. All of it was paid for by Leonid. Down below on the pavement, Skelly, Quince's tall, skinny Jamaican friend, was making jerk pork while his wife fussed with the side dishes, rice and beans and collard greens; a full plate went for three bucks.

The music, mostly hip-hop and rap, wafted across the Anacostia River, across the Moat, into DC proper, towards Capitol Hill, across the Mall, maybe even rebounding against the Lincoln Memorial, across the Ellipse and into Clinton's White House. But probably not.

The cops passed by a couple of times; the cops didn't say shit. No need to start a riot. No one was complaining about the music except for the few old biddies who were still fighting with the DJ over it. One would pull on his shirtsleeve, asking for some Fifties jazz, and five minutes later the old biddie's *grandma* would start in anew, turning the clock back yet again: 'Play some Chester Burnett!'

'Who's that, now?'

'Howlin' Wolf, you cowboy! I need to hear me some blues!'

Quince approached Leonid, who was sitting alone on the curb, fingering his new ring and watching these strangers spend his money. 'What're you doin', man?' he exclaimed. 'Why're you sittin' there all by your lonesome?'

'I am not big party person.'

'Bullshit! C'mon, get out there and shake it, baby! Meet some sistas! You hearing me?'

Leonid looked up. 'I did not know you have sister.'

Quince burst out laughing. For him, as well as most everyone else in the area who knew their new Russian neighbour, Leonid was a non-stop comedy jam.

'Leo, you are all kinds of crazy, you know that? You kill me, man! Yeah, sure I got a sister, two of 'em, in fact, and you better keep your damn hands off 'em, too. But that's not who I'm talkin' about. I'm talkin' about *sistas*, not "sisters"! You dig women, right?'

'I am only sleeping with women, I think you mean.'

'Yeah, dawg! That's *exactly* what I mean! Tell me somethin', man, when was the last time you got some?'

'Pussy, you are meaning, yes?'

'Yes, man! Pussy, goddamit!'

'Was in Dresden, Germany, on vacation. In 1993, in summer.'

'Whoa, whoa, whoa! Back the fuck up, man! *Nineteen ninety-three?!* You know what fuckin' year this is, here?'

'Is 1996. Yes, I know. I told you, was in war zone, refugee camp, not have time for fuck.'

'That's just excuses, now! You said that was for a few months. Now you're talkin' about three whole years! And why Germany, man? You Russian right, how come you wasn't tapping all that sweet Commie ass?'

'Can not trust Russian woman. Only want money.'

'Dawg, that be all women!'

'Maybe you are right in this, Quince.' Leonid took a swig off his forty. 'Maybe you are correct.'

'Hey, now, don't go getting all down on me, man. That's just the way it is, no use cryin' about it. Anyway, you got a good job over across the Moat, hell, you're *payin'* for all this out here! Women love that shit, man!'

'OK.'

'C'mon, get up. I got someone in mind for you. A higher class of woman, if you know what I mean. C'mon.'

Leonid stood up grudgingly and followed Quince through the crowd. *I'm too old for this shit.*

It was true. Even though he was only verging on his thirtieth year, Chechnya had done a number on him – he was only now just realizing it. Being there, being in the war, was different. He lived day to day, moment to moment. Now that he was safe, seemingly safe in America, he was feeling the effects. Although he felt all his troubles were behind him now, that he was in a 'Golden Age' of sorts, he still also felt like a Golden Ager, a senior citizen. *Maybe I'll just move down to Florida in a few years. I hear that's what they do. I'll just lie on the fucking beach, drinking until my liver explodes. Or until the tide takes me out.*

But when he saw the woman to whom Quince intended to introduce him, a spring came back into his step immediately. All thought of death left him. Quince made the intros, building Leonid up a bigshot. 'Yo, Ameshika, I'd like you to meet the man of the hour. This here is Leo, who organized this whole shebang tonight.'

'Oh, yeah, I've been hearing a whole lot about him. How'd you afford all this here tonight, Leo? You rob banks or something?'

Leonid shook her hand, smiling politely. 'No, no banks. Not as for yet.'

'Ain't he something! Listen, baby, you mind if I leave the man here with you? I got some business needs lookin' after.'

'No problem. We're cool.' She did not let go of his hand, and looked him directly in the eye. The last time someone had looked at Leonid like that, he'd had a gun to his head. This was somehow different.

'Your name, it is beautiful.'

'Well, thank you kindly, sir.'

'What is the significance?'

'How ever do you mean?'

She was still holding his hand, looking at him unblinkingly and flashing a thousand-watt smile. Leonid was now beginning to sweat, and a long-neglected part of him was disturbing the keys in his trouser pockets.

'Ah, I mean, what is the meaning? As my name means "lion", yours will mean …?'

'Are you a lion, Leo?'

'Ah, a lion is a cat, yes?'

'Yes, Leo.'

'And you call cat also "pussy", yes?'

'Yes, Leo.'

'OK. Then I am lion.'

Ameshika finally broke her gaze and released his hand to laugh. This relaxed Leonid a bit. He was not nearly drunk enough yet for such high-intensity flirting.

'So what about "Ameshika"? What is meaning?'

'My name, baby, means "human gold". So what do you think of that?'

At this, Leonid did not so much think as remember. He was suddenly back on the E55 with Vlatsky and the whores again for a moment, then returned quickly.

'"Human gold" ...? I like this. What is language?'

'It's Ewe, from Ghana. *Shika* means "gold", *ame* means "person" or "human". You know Ghana?'

'I am not familiar with this.'

'It's my country.'

'Country? You are not American?'

'I am ... but I'm not.'

'How do you mean?'

'Well, really, baby, there aren't any Americans excepting, of course, your Indian man. Everyone else up in here is relocated.'

'They did not come of own accord, yes?'

'Some did – the rich did – but most came for reasons beyond their control.'

'What reasons?'

'Fateful reasons. By means not of their own choosing. Never let anyone tell you they came here by choice. That's bullshit! That's a ruse!'

'We did not come here of choice?'

Ameshika was becoming fiery now. 'Hell, no! We just came! In my case, as in my name, it was a story of human gold!'

'What about my case? I want for come here.'

'You need to answer that for yourself; I'm not the one to do it.'

'I am answering. My whole life, I want for come here.'

'No, you didn't. You only thought you did. You probably should have stayed exactly where you were.'

'But it was a hell!'

'Hey baby, no one said it would be easy.'

Suddenly a big man Leonid had not seen before approached the couple, interrupting their conversation. He looked Leonid up and down.

'Who's this then, huh? Who's this you getting all cosy with, over here? Who is this motherfucker?'

'Why don't you get back to your baby's mother and leave me be, man! Just leave me be!'

'Why you gotta bring that shit up for, huh?'

Ameshika retorted, and then he said his piece, and she said hers, and on and on it went. Leonid stood there, nonchalant, drinking from his forty. *This guy is an absolute shithead.*

Ameshika finally made a formal introduction. 'Look Rick, you wanna know who this is, this is Leonid. Leonid, this bitch is Rick.'

'Hello, bitch,' said Leonid.

The man's eyes widened. 'What the *fuck* did you just say to me?!'

'Ah, I say wrong. Hello, bitch Rick.'

'You *playin'*? Are you playin' with me?!'

'I am sure I am not.' Leonid paused briefly for another swig, and then continued: 'Play how?'

Rick looked back at Ameshika, who was doubled over with laughter. 'Who – is – this – mother – fucker ...?' he snarled.

'Please for not call me by this name again. My mother, she is dead in ground.'

'*Fuck* your mother!' Rick shouted, and began poking Leonid in the chest and speaking slowly: 'You need to stay away from this bitch! You hearing me? You got that?'

Ameshika quickly corrected him, incensed. 'I'm not your "bitch", Rick! I ain't your woman, either. Never have been!' Rick's eyes went wide again.

'Yes, I am feeling too that you are mistaken, bitch Rick. Nobody belong to nobody else. Sure, maybe in past, but now not so. In Russia we understand about *Amerikanski* slavedom and slave mentality. Learn in school.'

Rick was frothing now: 'Who're you calling a *slave*, boy?!'

'I am not saying "slave". Headshit, maybe, but not slave. You are free man to be headshit, I am thinking.'

'Who the *fuck* do you think you're calling a headshit?!'

Quince noticed the scene starting up, and ran straight over. 'Rick, what are you doing, man?' he said as he intervened. 'Chill!'

'What am I doing!? This mother calling me a headshit, and you're asking me what I'm doing!?'

'Rick ... man, this is Leonid. From Russia, man. He's our host here tonight. Don't go fucking up the party, now.'

'Well, what's he doin' with my woman over here?'

'Rick, that's your woman over there,' said Quince, gesturing towards somewhere in the crowd, 'with your baby. Now step off.'

Rick backed down reluctantly and walked off towards his family, dejected and shaking his lowered head.

'You two alright?' Quince asked Leonid and Ameshika.

'No problem. Met many headshits before.'

Quince laughed again and went back to his business.

'You are a very interesting man, Leonid,' Ameshika smiled. 'Very interesting.'

'I am not sure I am liking this word "very" too much, this "interesting" also.'

'Why not?'

'Somebody tell me Chinese curse that said this: "You should live in the interesting times." Is not a good thing this. *Less* interesting is better. More calm.'

'That's a good one. There are some headshits up here I need to holler that one out to. They'll probably think it's something out of a damn Hallmark Christmas card.' With this, Ameshika led him out to dance amongst the parked cars in the street, to a tune by Al Green, *Tired of Being Alone*.

Fred and Quince watched the pair slow dance, looking quite pleased with themselves. Quince said: 'I told you she'd go for him, man.'

Fred nodded, full of fondness for this Russian. 'How are we doing on that other surprise?'

'It's lookin' good. The jug is near to bursting with cake.'

'Let's hand it over after church on Sunday. Maybe I can get it filled up a bit more. And Leo don't strike me as the kindo to handle any kind of public-speaking-type gig too well.'

'Alright then, my man. We'll lug it all over to him Sunday afternoon.'

By the end of the night, the block party was generally considered a great success. Everyone had eaten and drunk their fill; people of all ages had had the chance to dance to their kind of music; some people even got laid that night. The police kept out of it, and nobody got shot in Anacostia for a change.

❂

Leonid was not one of the many who'd gotten laid after the block party. He and Ameshika had fooled around on the dance floor, however, and arranged a dinner date for the following week. Leonid was grateful that she had slowed things down. He wasn't quite sure he could even seal the deal, after so much time spent celibate. Who knew what was going on down there in his pants?

Worn out, he had pretty much blown off the Saturday after the party; he'd woken up late, watched some bad television and ordered up some Pendeli's, and that was his day.

He slept in on Sunday too, until an insistent knocking brought him to. He opened the door to find Fred, Quince and Oz beaming at him. 'Why for so happy?' he asked, groggily.

'Wake up, son,' Fred said as he barged in. 'Fetch us some drinks.' He called back to Quince and Oz: 'Bring it on up in here.'

The other two carried in a huge jug, and as they plopped it down on the floor, it made a rattling sound.

Leonid peered in and saw coins and paper money of several denominations. 'What is this?'

'We turned the party into a sort of charity event, Leo,' said Fred. 'Everybody chipped in. This here, this is for you. Now, where're those drinks at? These boys must've worked up a powerful thirst carrying this up four floors.'

Quince and Oz nodded in agreement.

Leonid replied, bewildered: 'Only have vodka in home. Is OK?'

'Yeah! Pour out four!' Fred was jubilant. 'This calls for a celebration!'

Leonid poured out the drinks and said: *'Nostrovya.'* They all clinked glasses, and then Fred explained: 'All this, in this jug, is for you, Leo. For all the good you've done in this neighbourhood. You understand?'

Leonid's eyes grew glassy. He understood. Then he turned to Quince. 'This is surprise you talked of.'

Quince grinned. 'See, everybody knows what you did for this building, man,' Quince replied. 'We all know you sunk a helluva lot a bills into this improvement. Did you think we weren't gonna say thanks?'

Leonid looked directly at him, but couldn't find words. The other three men laughed nervously.

'That's the surprise we planned on,' continued Quince. 'Only you yourself know how the other one went ...' He laughed. Leonid understood that he meant Ameshika, though she was not a gift one could make. He had to turn away. He was overwhelmed by these acts, these gestures made – not for the first time – by people who were veritable strangers to him His memory was improving now, and he began playing with his ring. He also began to weep, silently. All he could summon up to say was: 'We order from Pendeli's.'

Quince said: 'Me and Oz will go get some forties to wash that down with.' They left Fred with Leonid. The older man said nothing, and dialled up the pizza place while Leonid continued to weep. Fred had the gift for simple silence that comes with age.

❁

The following Monday, Leonid was outside the sauna, promptly as usual. But 9.30 had come and gone, and the always-punctual and predictable Sarkhov was nowhere to be seen. Leonid gave him fifteen more minutes before deciding to go in and check things out for himself.

He entered the humid building and paid the entrance fee. Beyond the locker rooms were the two main sauna rooms, one dry and the other wet. Leonid stuck his head into each, and thought he recognized Sarkhov's form through the thick mist of the wet sauna. He approached the tiled, bleacher-like seats and noticed two men, one was performing fellatio on the other while wanking his own cock. Leonid looked away. *Those idiots are going to have heart attacks doing that stuff in here!*

When he got close enough to the figure he believed might be Sarkhov, he realized the man was rubbing one out too: he gave Leonid a knowing, come-hither look – but it was not Sarkhov. Leonid left the room and searched further. Beyond the saunas there were several private rooms. He knocked on a few of them, calling out Sarkhov's name, receiving grunting, pre-orgasmic 'Wrong room!'s and 'Not here!'s. Someone even yelled out: *'¡Occupado, pendejo!'*

Finally, one door was opened to him. He was pulled in by one of three naked men, all sporting wood. A fourth was handcuffed to a bed with rubber sheets. This was Sarkhov.

The first thing that caught Leonid's eye was the intricate ankle-to-neck tattoo work on the man's naked body, all symbols of his status in the Mafiya going back to the postwar gulags. He ran his eyes from bottom to top … and that's when he noticed another element in the rich tapestry of this man's life: he had faecal matter all over his mouth. *Om mani padme hum!* Leonid tried to keep his composure.

'Who is this guy, Sharky, huh?' growled one of the men. 'I thought we had a deal. We don't need a fifth wheel here!'

'Not for worry. Stay on four wheels. I am just driver.'

'What is that supposed to mean? You want to get behind my wheel?'

Leonid ignored the remark and switched to Russian, addressing Sarkhov, trying not to gag: 'I am sorry for interrupting, sir. I was concerned because it's almost 10.00. Usually we leave at 9.30.'

'I seem to have gotten carried away. My apologies. Give me a half-hour.'

'Carried away', is it! You're eating shit in here! 'As you wish, sir. I'll be out front.' Leonid turned to make his exit.

'Yeah, get the fuck out of here!' screamed one of the men.

'You can believe on that one,' Leonid replied, using an expression he had learned from Quince. 'I am like ghost!'

Leonid was already on his fifth drink by the time Sarkhov had cleaned himself up and exited the sauna. He didn't even bother to hide the vodka, nor did he open the rear passenger door for the man. Sarkhov sat himself down and Leonid peeled the Cadillac towards the embassy. An air of tension suffused the car.

Sarkhov decided to break the silence and spoke to Leonid at length for the second time since he had hired him as his driver: 'Forget the embassy today. Just take me home. We'll call it a day.' Leonid remained silent and changed course.

Sarkhov spoke again: 'You should not have had to see that.'

Leonid, trembling, could not restrain himself: 'See what? I think I went blind in there!'

'You don't understand. I can see that. But you work for me, and you know it must remain a secret between us. Now pass me back one of those "little waters" you're drinking up there.'

Leonid reached into his coat pocket and passed back an airplane bottle of vodka to Sarkhov. He noticed an inkblot of a prison tattoo, crudely etched between thumb and forefinger, stretched forth to him. *Shit stain?* He was careful not to touch the man's hand. Sarkhov grabbed the bottle and downed it in a gulp.

Despite the warnings he had been given about Sarkhov, Leonid heard himself continue: 'I've seen a lot of bad and crazy things in my life, but this …!'

Sarkhov retorted furiously: 'This *what*? What do you think you've seen that I haven't? Tell me!'

'Is that how your last driver ended up dead?' Leonid's voice rose a few notches.

'Stop shouting. Calm yourself. The other driver died because he tried to cheat me. This is different. Listen. Leonid. I like you. You must be discreet, do you understand? If this got out …'

'I won't say anything. I wouldn't even know how to begin.'

'I must have your word.'

'Yes. Yes, you have it.' Leonid was calming down. He needed this job after all. He also wanted to live.

'Good. And in the future, if I'm late coming out, just wait in the car.'

'I won't make that mistake again.' Leonid paused, then pressed his luck once again: 'Just tell me, please ... why do you do ... *that?*'

'What can I tell you? It relaxes me. It's that simple.'

Leonid dropped Sarkhov off at his K Street address. As he pulled back out into traffic, he thought about what Sarkhov's last words might mean. What was eating him, that an activity such as swallowing the faeces of others would relax him? Then he thought about his own method of relaxation.

He decided his was better. He dropped off the car at the garage, went home and got as drunk as possible, in an effort to forever erase from his mind the image of Sarkhov doing his thing; in an effort, too, to erase the vast array of other images he had accumulated over the years. But it wasn't working. The imagery was always stronger than the drink.

TWELVE

Leonid passed a long and restless night plagued with shit-eating dreams. His alarm went off at 7.00 AM, saving him from more of the same.

He had just finished his breakfast and was about to head out the door when his phone rang. It was Andrei, calling from New York. 'Leonid, I'm glad I caught you. Do you have time to talk?'

Here it comes. Om mani padme hum. 'I have a few minutes,' he said cautiously, before adding: 'You know Mr Sarkhov's policy regarding punctuality, of course.'

'Yes, yes, I certainly do. That's why I'm calling, actually.'

'Oh, really?' *I'm dead! Oh fuck, am I dead!*

'He called me last night. He wanted to know all about your personal history.'

How will they do it? How will they kill me? Will I see the bullet coming? I hope not.

'He was that pleased with your performance. I hope you don't mind, but I was compelled to reveal your travails in Chechnya. All that bad business with Miki and Borzoi. I apologize, but he is my superior, and …'

'No need, Andrei, none at all.' Leonid couldn't believe what he was hearing.

'Well, when I finished relating your story, I can tell you he was more than a little impressed.'

'Why? Why should that impress him?'

'Because, my friend, you are a survivor. If you understood Sarkhov's psychology, it would be clear to you. Listen, I should let you go. But before I do, let me warn you: he'll have a surprise for you today.'

'I … I don't like surprises,' Leonid whimpered.

'Of course you do. Everyone likes a surprise.' With that, Andrei disconnected the line, leaving Leonid trembling. He was getting mixed messages, and had been left with no idea where he stood with Sarkhov. He took five long shnorts off a bottle of vodka before leaving for work.

❂

Sarkhov exited the sauna promptly at 9.30. Leonid was at the ready, car door open. He drove Sarkhov over to the Russian embassy. Not a word passed between them. As Leonid waited in the car, he thought of Andrei's comments. He was right – this was a surprise. Sarkhov was acting as though the previous day never had happened. As though all had been forgotten.

The day continued as usual. Sarkhov had his lunch date at an upscale Chinese restaurant; Leonid had his street-vendor hotdogs in the car. Afterwards, he was instructed to drive to several business addresses around town, at which Sarkhov spent no more than thirty minutes each. Then, the workday finished, it was time to go home. Leonid made his way over to K Street, battling traffic.

When he parked, Sarkhov motioned him to stay where he was, in the driver's seat, and then produced a small, hand-carved wooden box. Inside the box, which was lined in velvet, was a Luger semi-automatic pistol. Sarkhov removed it and fondled it gently, as Leonid watched through the rear-view mirror.

Leonid was sweating now. Like an idiot, he had returned his Glock to the glove compartment at the last stop, figuring the day was over. Now Sarkhov had the drop on him. He was dead. He didn't even bother with his short Buddhist prayer; it was all over. And for nothing more than witnessing a man eating shit.

'Do you know what this is?' Sarkhov spoke calmly and very evenly.

Just pull the trigger already!

'When I was fifteen years old, the Party gang-pressed me into the infantry. I was big for my age, but still very much a child. "The Great Patriotic War", as they called it, had turned, and the push towards Berlin was in full throttle. I was amongst the forces that took the city. We had been encouraged to take our revenge, and we raped every woman we came upon; my own commanding officer even ordered us to do so.'

Who cares! Just do the job and shoot! I don't need reasons!

'I did my part very well. It was difficult at first, but one got used to it. One developed the taste for it. I must have raped hundreds of Germans. This Luger belonged to an SS captain. My unit had captured him and his family. I fucked his wife while he watched, at gunpoint. Fucked her in the ass, too. We all did. Just to make sure he got the point. Then we did the same to his eldest daughter. He had a son and another daughter, too, prepubescent; we fucked them both as well. And then we killed them with this Luger. We let the other two women live so they would come to term and bear our children. When I saw that the Nazi had seen all he thought he could bear, when the light went out of his eyes, I fucked him in the ass also, and then I blew his brains out with his own gun. This Luger.'

At this point, Leonid considered starting up the car again and driving it into oncoming traffic.

'When Germany was finally destroyed, broken in half, we drank with the Americans who had come from the other direction. It was like Nero's Rome. The city was in ruins, and we drank and screwed while it burned. Stalin eventually relieved us and brought us back to the Motherland – but not as free men. So many of us who had come to see the end of the war at the Western front, we were sent to the gulags.'

Leonid had never heard any of this before. He remained silent.

'I managed to get this gun, this souvenir, to my mother before my imprisonment. In prison, with people who had seen and done what I myself had participated in, well, let me just tell you, we were changed men already … but in prison we changed even more. Our tastes changed. Just to give you an idea of the extremes, they even ran to cannibalism.

'It was in these gulags that the modern Mafiya was established. It was all about survival. Survival amongst each other took the idea further: we had to survive the Communists on the outside, and each other on the inside. This was the genesis of the network today, you understand?'

Leonid understood all too well.

'You,' Sarkhov continued, 'are one of us. I know what that animal Borzoi put you through. Still, you survived.'

Borzoi is the animal now?

'And now you live down there in Anacostia, with the blacks. Correct?'

'Yes.'

'I admire that. It will keep you sharp. Most of the men who work for me wouldn't last down there for five minutes.' Sarkhov paused for a long while before he spoke again: 'That's why I'm giving you this Luger.' With that, he passed the gun in its box up to Leonid. 'It is a symbol of our likeness. Our bond.'

Leonid could only think: *Look at this! I've been in this country for just a few months, never having owned a gun before; now I have three!*

Stunned, he accepted the gun, thanked Sarkhov and came around to open the door for him. Then, as Sarkhov disappeared into his building, he thought long and hard about quitting the Mafiya and finding a normal job. Maybe even a job down at the Pizza Hut with Fred. One in which your boss didn't send you on suicide missions. One in which your boss didn't feel the need to devour faecal matter in order to absolve himself of past sins.

Leonid would break yet another Mafiya rule: he ceased to give a damn. Taking the Cadillac out of the parking garage for his big date with Ameshika, he drove it over the Moat back into Anacostia and picked up Quince. Leonid had arranged a deal with Quince to drive him, with Ameshika, to dinner at some posh French bistro in Georgetown, a place he knew Sarkhov frequented. He was trying to make an impression.

Quince wanted to know more about the car, but Leonid silenced him with an extra fifty dollars, adding that he had a rich uncle. Quince was suspicious, but went along with the story. 'You want me to open up the door for y'all and such?'

'*Nyet*. No need. I will be working on door situation. Just drive car. Here is twenty dollars more for get food. Just be sure you are in front of place by 9.30, yes?'

'Don't sweat it, my man. You need to chill. Women smell that fear, eat a man up for breakfast!'

Quince was right. They hadn't even gone yet to pick up Ameshika, and Leonid was already sweating copiously. 'Oh my God! How I do this thing?'

'I told you to chill! All you need to do is treat her like a lady. That's it! Just keep it simple. Keep the bullshit out of it, you follow?'

'Yes. Am following.'

'Alright, then. Next thing: don't tell her the truth. Lie your damn ass off. About every damn thing!'

'You just told me not for to bullshit?'

'That ain't the same, man! You need to learn English! What I'm saying is, don't let her know how bad y'all want to get your end in, and the good Lord knows you do! But *she* can't know that! She's the one that's got to want you. She's gotta feel in control. You seeing my point here?'

'OK. So I am lying about want for sex. What am I telling truth on?'

'Nothing, man! Whatever she wants to hear, whatever you feel she needs to hear, that's the shit you tell her!'

'But I think she want for make eventual sex with me. So I should say this, yes?'

'No, man! Never! Even when you're bangin' her, shut your mouth about it. She needs to be the one wanting the fuckin'! Not you!'

'You are putting me into a great confusion now.' Leonid was becoming more anxious.

'No I ain't, Leo.' Quince had to laugh. 'I seen you at work. You got the gift.'

'Gift?'

'Yeah, man, the gift. You're full of shit! You just go on ahead and lie to her like you lied to me about these here cool fuckin' wheels. You just do that, and you might get laid tonight.'

❋

'Well, aren't you the bigshot!' said Ameshika as she took a seat on the chair Leonid held out for her once they had been shown to their table.

'Why for this are you saying?'

'Well, everything. Having Quince drive us over in that sweet ride. This place. Everything.'

'You like, yes?'

She smiled. 'A girl could get used to this.'

A waiter came and took their orders, and Leonid requested an expensive wine – not necessarily a good one, just an expensive one. He didn't know wine.

'So, Leo, if you don't mind my asking, how does a guy like you, living in the ghetto, afford all this here? Don't get me wrong: it's all good. I'm just curious. Damn, my last man used to think hopping on a bus and scarfing down some Denny's was the height of a romantic evening!'

Leonid, sticking to his rule about not mentioning the Mafiya, deflected the question: 'Not for to get used to it. I am only for making big impression upon you.'

Ameshika laughed. 'You just never stop, do you! You just might be the funniest man I have ever met!'

'Is so. Next date at Denny's. You are the one to pay.'

'Ha! So it's gonna be like that, huh?'

When Leonid asked her in turn what she did for work, she replied: 'I'm what you might call an entrepreneur. I design my own jewellery and sell it out of a shop I run.'

'So you are rich merchant! I let you pay this one too, then.'

Here Ameshika laughed again, softly and more wickedly. 'You gonna have me pay for it, hmm?' She slipped a foot out of her shoe, and caressed Leonid's calf with it, sliding it up his leg to the knee. Leonid called the waiter back with some urgency, and ordered a triple vodka.

'You want same?'

'I don't need vodka to get juicy,' Ameshika replied mischievously.

'Hurry up with vodka!' Leonid half-screamed at the waiter. This woman was killing him.

'You look nervous, Leo,' she said. 'Is that it – are you just a bundle of nerves?'

'Let me for to explain,' Leonid replied. 'You say to keep it slow at party, I am agreeing with this ideal. Has been long time for me since ... making sex with woman. Needing some time more. You are understanding, yes?'

Ameshika nodded and removed her foot slowly. 'I do, Leo. You know, I do not meet many guys out there who wouldn't try and have me under this table by this point ... *That's* what's impressing me, more than anything.'

Maybe Quince knew what he was talking about after all. I have her! Leonid smiled at her, silently. His vodka came and he downed it, trying to kill his hard-on.

'The car is belonging to a rich uncle of mine. I say this because you asked.'

❁

The promise of sex with Ameshika, combined with Quince's questions regarding his last lay and Sarkhov's depraved stories, sent Leonid into a mood of thoughtful remembrance, back to Hamburg in 1993: the last time he had, to use Quince's phrase, got his end in.

He and Vlatsky had been taking a week off from pimping. They had dropped off some girls at a whorehouse in Prague, and were having a shnort over at a *hospoda* called *U vystřelenýho oka* in the late afternoon. Vlatsky, out of the clear blue sky, had mentioned The Beatles. 'I want to listen to Beatle music,' was how he put it. 'I'm very fond of that group.'

'Go ahead then,' Leonid said. 'I'm sure they have a cassette tape at the bar. Go ask them.'

'No, it's not the same. I need to hear it live.'

'Live! How drunk are you? They're all dead, aren't they?'

'Only one is dead, you idiot! Paul McCartney! Don't you remember the line "I buried Paul"? Now listen to me: we can be in Hamburg in seven hours. Nearly half that, if I'm driving.'

'Why Hamburg?' asked Leonid.

'You've never been there? The Reeperbahn? That's where they started out. They have Beatle revival bands over there every five minutes!'

'But I thought they were British.'

'Of course they were British! But they couldn't get laid in Liverpool, so they went to Germany, where the girls love to fuck. Don't you know anything?'

Leonid agreed to make the drive to Hamburg with Vlatsky – but only after a few more drinks.

Vlatsky's claims about driving time proved more than false, what with all the roadside stops required for the purpose of throwing back more drinks. They arrived in Hamburg shortly before 1.00 AM and headed straight for the Reeperbahn. Even then, it took them another hour to find a Beatles revival show on the boulevard; but they did, much to Leonid's amazement.

The group continued to perform for another hour. Vlatsky drank St Pauli Girl beers, his eyes closed in appreciation, trying to picture the actual Beatles singing his favourites. Leonid drank vodka.

Then it happened: the group performed their rendition of *Back in the USSR*, and Leonid lost it. He knew the song from way back, and had always held it as a jerky idea of a capitalist's apology to Mother Russia; but that was before his eyes were opened, before his father's tours in Afghanistan and resultant brain damage, before a television exploded in his mother's face, before her suicide and even before the Wall came down. One of the things that song *hadn't* come before was the Mafiya; the other was the threat of all-out nuclear war. Leonid heard the lyrics now in a new light, and his eyes welled up with tears.

'... back in the USSR/You don't know how lucky you are, boy ...'

A slap in the face: Leonid had wanted America.

'Been away so long I hardly knew the place ...'

He wanted to be away for good. *Fuck you, the Beatles! Fuck you!* He knew the place. Too well.

(There were other lines in there to upset him, but only from the perspective of a future that he did not know at that point: lyrics such as *That Georgia's always on my my my my my my my my mind*, which now would make him remember Eva's death, and Hanson's, too. And lastly: *Oh, show me round your snow-peaked mountains way down south*, which would remind him of everything that had gone down in the Caucasus, the bloody hell he had been through.)

What he didn't know was that a girl in the club had been observing all his reactions to the song. She had noticed him earlier with some interest, but now she was intrigued, and decided to make her approach.

'*Warum bist Du am Weinen wenn Du das Lied hoerst?*'

'I am not speaking the German.'

She understood, and rephrased the question in English: 'Why do you cry when you hear this song? You look very sad.'

'I am coming from Russia.'

✿

The girl, Laura, invited Leonid and Vlatsky to join her at a beer hall around the corner after the show, where she had plans to meet some friends. Vlatsky declined, citing his need to black out: 'I'm going to catch a taxi and have him drop me at some fleabag hotel,' he told Leonid. 'Remember where the car is parked. We'll meet exactly here, at this club, at 5 PM.'

They each wrote down the name of the club on scraps of paper and put them in their wallets: tricks of the trade for alcoholics visiting strange towns. Vlatsky bid Laura and Leonid farewell, and was off.

Leonid went with Laura to the beer hall and met her friends, but really only spoke with her for the remainder of the night. She explained that she was from behind the Iron

Curtain too, having been born in Dresden in the German Democratic Republic – the former East Germany.

'I understand your sadness,' she told him.

'Was bad for you too, yes?'

'It was. But it's a new world now.'

She spoke with great enthusiasm about how she and her friends had been in Berlin when the Wall came down, how strangers from East and West Germany alike had embraced each other and wept tears of joy, how they partied for days on end.

Leonid saw things a bit differently. Maybe it was a new world, but that didn't mean it was a better one. He kept his pessimism to himself, though. Even though he had known her only for a few hours, he already thought he might be falling in love with this girl; he didn't want to risk turning her off with his sour visions.

She led him into a private corner, away from the others, and kissed him passionately.

'Shall we go back to my hotel?'

'Hotel? I thought you are living here.'

'No, I'm just visiting. I still live in Dresden.'

Leonid drove her to the hotel. It was quite far out of the city centre, somewhere in the suburbs. He had no idea where he was going, and lost his way several times – not a good thing when aching for sex. His frustration came shining through: 'Who for invent these streets! It is making no sense! Have not landmarks, have not bars, even!'

Laura put her arm on his and tried to calm him. 'If you listen to me, you will not get lost,' she said. Her voice soothed and relaxed him. She told him where to go. He followed, and they arrived.

They both awoke late the next day. Her back turned to him, Leonid watched Laura breathe, exhilarated, and tried to remember how many times they had gone at it. He had to stop at five – beyond that, he couldn't be sure. He had surprised himself.

Laura rolled over to face him and smiled. 'What are you thinking?'

'That we are winning gold Olympic medal last night.'

She laughed. 'Was that not normal for you?'

Leonid thought of Vlatsky's comment on the reason the Beatles had moved to Germany: *These girls really do love to fuck!* Suddenly he was hard again.

'Normal? I'll show you for normal!' With that, he reached out for her; she was all for it. But then he saw the bedside clock, which read 4.47 PM. 'Holy shit!' he shouted in Russian, leaping up. 'Vlatsky!'

Leonid drove furiously, but not without taking Laura's direction. She agreed to come along and help him not get lost on the way back to the club. They arrived at 5.30 PM, but the club had not yet opened and they found Vlatsky sleeping on a bench in front of it and looking like shit – but that was nothing new.

Leonid shook him awake. 'Come on, Vlatsky! It's time to go!'

'Go where, you merciless pig? I'm on vacation. Let me sleep.'

'Get off that fucking bench! You look homeless. Should I drop a *kopek* in your hand?'

That riled Vlatsky enough to put him upright. Laura didn't understand the two Russians, but still found the scene hilarious. Vlatsky looked at his watch, then smiled at Laura and switched to English: 'The two lovers are late.' Laura blushed.

'What happened, you layabout?' asked Leonid.

'I couldn't get a taxi, so I made myself comfortable here. What's the difference ... Are we ready to go back to Prague?'

Leonid looked at Laura. 'We still have time off, Vlatsky. Why not hang around?'

Thus they decided to stay on in Hamburg for another day before Laura had to return to work in Dresden. However, she invited them both to make the four-hour trip from Hamburg and meet in Dresden, until they had to get back to their own jobs. Leonid and Vlatsky could stay at her place, she added. Dresden was only two hours away from Prague – along the E55. They agreed, and it was during dinner at Laura's that the subject of work finally came up.

'So,' said Laura, 'you two work together?'

Leonid and Vlatsky exchanged looks. Vlatsky took the lead: 'Yes. We are truck drivers.'

'And Prague will be your first stop?'

'Yes. We must collect some cargo there, Sunday.'

'Where will you deliver it?'

Leonid still had not said a word. He was nervously shovelling food in his mouth and sweating, unsure what Vlatsky would say.

'We are driving it up north to the docks at Gdansk.'

'Ah, in Poland.' She looked over at Leonid, and took his hand. 'I was hoping maybe you will be returning to Germany.'

Leonid gulped some food down, a little relieved. 'We will. It is changing, the job, every time. But we are coming to Germany many times. Is not so, Vlatsky?'

'We travel through here a lot, yes.'

Laura smiled, leaned over and kissed Leonid deeply. Vlatsky broke it up before it became X-rated. He had been kipping on Laura's sofa for the past few nights, and had heard them constantly in the bedroom. The poor man couldn't sleep. 'Laura,' he said, we still do not know your job. Where do you disappear, in the morning?'

'I work for the government, doing investigations. It is boring to tell, really. I sit in my office all day, reading documents, searching for facts. But it's still very personal to me.'

'Why?' Leonid asked.

'It is part of the reunification of this country. I read transcripts, records of false confessions made to the Stasi, the Ministry for State Security of the DDR: the East German secret police.'

Almost in unison, Vlatsky and Leonid looked at each other and – said: 'KGB.'

'Yes, like those assholes. *Diese Arschlöcher.*' Laura suddenly grew very emotional, and her eyes misted.

'What is wrong, *golubushka?*'

'I am sorry. Both my parents disappeared during Stasi interrogations. They took them – my father first, and then two weeks later, my mother. I never saw them again. I was fifteen at the time. I belonged to the State after that.' She looked at Leonid and pulled his hand to her cheek. 'That's why I approached you at the club, *Liebchen*. Watching your reaction to that song, I felt like I knew everything inside of you. I knew I was in love.'

Now Leonid was tearing up as well. She was everything he ever wanted – and everything he wanted to be: an orphan. 'I am loving you too,' he replied.

Vlatsky excused himself discreetly and went out in search of a bar.

✸

Now that the floodgates had opened wide, conversations between the couple ran back and forth between topics such as their shared hatred of totalitarianism to their great love for each other. And then Sunday came, and it was time for Leonid and Vlatsky to depart for Prague. To collect some cargo. Laura gave Vlatsky a double-cheeked kiss before taking care of her man. Then, joking, she said the words that would drive Leonid away forever: 'Be sure not to catch something bad on the E55!' Vlatsky just laughed knowingly, but Leonid was startled by the remark.

'What do you know about this road?'

'The same thing that everybody knows. It is full of prostitutes.'

'How do you know of this?'

'You are joking, yes? Everyone knows that that whole motorway is run by the Mafiya. They're worse than the Communists! This is just another kind of slavery.'

And that was it. Leonid kissed her more passionately than he had done before that moment, and promised to call her as soon as he arrived. They were to meet again in two weeks, but they never met again. How could Leonid ever admit to her who he was, what he actually did for a living? She would despise him eternally.

Vlatsky pulled away from the pavement as Leonid waved goodbye and blew kisses from the car, tears wetting his face. When they had driven around the corner, Vlatsky stopped at a shop and got out. When he returned, it was with a bottle of vodka. He passed it over to Leonid, and Leonid took it.

Back in Georgetown, sitting across from the only other woman in over two years to have aroused such strong feelings in him, he remembered all this in detail. Once again, he resolved that no one – especially not Ameshika – would ever discover him for what he was.

On the night before Leonid was brought out of the emergency operating room of the Greater Southeast Community Hospital, with two bullets having been removed from his body – one of them mere millimetres from his spinal cord – and transferred safely to a private hospital for serious, long-term and expensive rehabilitation (to be covered, thankfully, by Mr Sarkhov's generosity), the following befell him.

It had been a night like any other. Leonid had returned from the day's work, gone straight to the freezer and grabbed one of many chilled vodka bottles stored within. He poured himself a glass and planted himself in front of the television.

During the news, he contemplated the problem of how to leave the Mafiya – unsuccessfully – and then dozed off. He awoke promptly as *Wheel of Fortune* came on the air, and was baffled to see a giant rat waving into the camera.

'Where is the Sajak?' he addressed the opening credits.

The game show was shooting on location at Disneyland, it turned out, and all the puzzles were connected to these special circumstances. Leonid caught on soon enough, and played along with the contestants – terribly, as usual. One clue fell under the category of 'Fictional Families'. He called out: 'The Romanovs!' and laughed heartily at his own little joke.

The next clue came up. Little by little, more letters appeared. Leonid jumped up and shouted: 'Is a small worry!' When the answer was revealed as IT'S A SMALL WORLD, he sat back down, dejected.

He continued playing until *Jeopardy* came on. If he sucked at *Wheel of Fortune*, then his performance during *Jeopardy* was a foregone conclusion. He used this half-hour time slot to make his thrice-weekly call to Pendeli's to order his dinner, giving them the time required to make the delivery before his next show came on at 8.00 PM. He could only ever eat in front of the television, even before America, even in Russia, even knowing the danger.

The people at Pendeli's knew him quite well, if by voice only, and greeted him warmly. He would hardly begin to order when they'd cut him off: 'Yeah, one large all-dressed with anchovies and red peppers instead of green, I know. I got you.'

He would then attempt to give his address, but again he would be interrupted: 'It'll be there in twenty minutes. Ciao.' And the line would go dead.

The American engine of efficiency never ceased to amaze him.

That taken care of, he'd turn on the radio to the same Top 20 station he always listened to, and pace around the flat, vodka in hand, musing about how good he had it. *Everything has fallen into place. Good woman, nice friends, good TV, acceptable plumbing, excellent pizza, father dead. The only thing left is to find a new job ... but what?*

It never occurred to Leonid that his was a life of dull routine, life by rote. Many people probably would have considered suicide as preferable – but then, such people had not experienced the Soviet Union, post-Communist Russia, Grozny during wartime and life in a refugee camp. So maybe, in Leonid's case, pizza and *Wheel of Fortune* would suffice.

❁

Down at Pendeli's, Leonid's pie was pulled out of the oven, ready to be boxed up and sent off. The delivery guy sat in the corner flipping through the pages of an old *People* magazine. Two fourteen-year-old youths sat on their bikes outside, waiting for him to start off.

As soon as the delivery guy came out with the pie and fired up his shitbox Chevette, the kids hit their bike pedals in hot pursuit.

Leonid heard the knock on the door. He had the money and tip prepared on a small table by the threshold. There was a single drawer in this table that held two of the three guns he owned.

He opened the door and greeted the delivery guy. They were both long acquainted with each other, and exchanged the usual pleasantries. Money and pizza swapped hands, followed by their goodbyes, and Leonid closed his door in anticipation of the dinner theatre ahead of him.

That's when he heard it: three muffled shots from the direction of the stairwell. He'd heard shots in the neighbourhood before, of course, but never in such close proximity.

Incautiously, he opened the door and found the two kids rifling through the delivery guy's pockets. If the delivery guy wasn't dead, he was sure doing a damn fine job of looking the part; the kids had opened up his third eye for him. Blood was spattered all over the hallway, and one of the kids was holding the money Leonid had just forked over. The other was holding a gun. They were so intent on their search that they didn't even notice Leonid, and he, for his part, just stood there watching dumbly, without reacting. At no time did it occur to him to reach into the drawer beside him and pull out one of his guns – the Luger or the .38 – and get some payback. This was, after all, his pizza delivery guy. This wasn't someone else's pizza delivery guy lying in a bloody mess out there, this was *his* fucking pizza delivery guy!

His neighbour from across the way, an elderly woman, opened her door a few seconds later and began screaming hysterically. Some of the delivery guy's brains were at her feet. Leonid came out of his daze, and the kids broke off their search. The woman locked her door and ran to the telephone, shouting: 'We'll see! Oh, hell yes, we gonna see when the police get here! Damn fools!'

The kids and Leonid made eye contact. Nobody flinched. The youth with the gun indicated to his friend to keep searching, and then put a bead on Leonid. Leonid was more concerned about what the hell else they were looking for than about the gun aimed at him. Truly, it troubled him. *They already have my money and the guy's wallet. What more could there be? What do these fuckers want?*

A jingling of keys answered him. The delivery guy's car keys had been located. The kid with the gun seemed satisfied: 'That's them. Let's roll, baby.'

The other kid bolted down the stairs, but the armed child spent a few more seconds staring at Leonid, each intrigued by the other. He made a silent-movie gesture with the gun, as though he had fired it, and said: 'Pow.' Then he, too, disappeared down the stairs.

Leonid closed the door and went to the window. He watched as the two kids threw their bikes in the hatchback and peeled out in the Chevette, on a joyride. Robotically, he poured out a fresh vodka, grabbed his all-dressed pizza with anchovies and red peppers instead of green, turned on his 8.00 programme and began to eat.

❂

About half an hour into his show and better than three-quarters through his pie, Leonid became aware of some rustling out in the stairwell. He rose from his chair and put an ear to the door; the rustling remained but rustling. He was still a long way from blocking out the earlier incident, and on this occasion decided to take precautions before opening his door. He opened the drawer in the table next to the threshold and selected the Luger. It was the only one of his three guns he was sure had killed in the past. This gave it a power over any and all comers. Gently, he opened the door, gun by his side, to find a policeman fumbling around his pizza delivery guy's body.

For this, he was promptly gutshot, twice.

✿

His mother was speaking to him now, kindly, as she always had done before the suicide. Her voice was subterranean, faint, but its meaning was clear: it wasn't anybody's fault, what had happened. Between her, her husband and their child, no one was to blame. He screamed back into the abyss that *all* were to blame. *Everybody on the fucking planet at any time in history was to fucking blame!*

'Poor child, don't blame your father,' was all he got back.

✿

The first sound Leonid heard when he came to was his elderly neighbour shouting: 'You stupid sons of bitches! You done shot the wrong man! I *told* you it was a coupla no-good little punks done the killin' 'round here! Your mama never teach you to listen to your elders?! That boy lying there is European, or some damn thing! He got our plumbin' fixed, and all! You ain't got no call for shooting him full of holes, god *damn* your asses!'

The cops were trying to push her back into her own flat and shut her up: 'Ma'am, please, now, this is a crime scene and we can't have all this commotion. Please ...'

'Commotion?! *Commotion?!* I got two dead bodies up in here and brains on my damn slippers, and you're talkin' about a commotion! Well, I never!'

'Please, Ma'am, bear with me, the detectives will be here directly to take your statement. If you would kindly just step back into your apartment.'

'Detectives, huh? Maybe I'll just tell them a little story about a cop shooting down a hero for nothing. Hell, yeah!'

❂

Leonid now found himself being wept over by a young rookie cop: 'I'm sorry, man! I'm so sorry! I thought you were drawing on me. But don't worry, there's an ambulance on the way. I don't know what to say ...'

Leonid took him for an idiot. Then he heard the rookie's partner, who was knelt beside him, try to calm him down: 'Listen, this wasn't your fault. This putz was holding a piece, and you shot him. End of story. In this neighbourhood, it don't mean a thing, ya got me? Self-defence. When the Chief asks, you just say "self-defence", and that's it, and that's all. Nothing more. It was a clean shoot!'

'But I ...'

'But you nothing! He had a piece! That's as good as gold!'

Leonid lifted an arm and pointed up at the table.

The rookie noticed this and asked: 'You want something here from the table, buddy? What are you looking for, pal?'

Leonid kept repeating the gesture, weakly. His finger was pointed somewhere between the remains of the pie and the remains of the vodka, but then it wilted, dropped and pointed at the useless remains of the pizza delivery guy.

The rookie decided Leonid wanted more pie, and handed him the box. Leonid found a burst of strength and knocked it from his hands. He pointed upwards again. This time, the rookie could make no mistake. It was the half-bottle of vodka the patient required.

The rookie passed it over and, after having a quick guzzle, Leonid pulled his shirt up and poured out some more liberally over his two wounds. He didn't even have to arch his neck to see them: he knew where they were without looking. His body was whole. He and his body had united.

After all these years of trying to disconnect from each other, they had finally become one.

After the cops observed him cleanse and stanch his wounds, watched him convulse from the pain, they felt it best to wrest the bottle from his hands. They could see he was going for yet another swig. Leonid disappeared back into the fog.

✸

Now it was Bill Hanson and his ring that came drifting into mind. Leonid never would have found himself in this fucking situation, had it not been for that ideologue. *Om mani padme hum.* Still, Hanson's voice called to him: 'It's all connected ... we're all connected.' As close as he reckoned he was to Jesus, St Peter *et al*, Leonid found Hanson's philosophy so devoid of any logic that it was laughable. Hanson called out, still: 'Each and every one of us can make the difference, small as it might be ...'

'I could not save him. I could not save even one,' sputtered Leonid as he returned to consciousness.

'Save who, buddy? Who you talking about?'

'What is pizza guy's name?'

'Huh?'

'What his fucking name is?!'

'Alright, hold on and I'll find out,' the rookie said. He walked over to the other cop and got his answer. Leonid watched from his worm's-eye view. He also saw the bottle and reached for it weakly, grabbing himself another shot.

'Was it Spaska?! Was his name fucking "Spaska!"?'

The rookie returned to Leonid's side. 'Uh, Spaska? What kind of name is that? No, his name was James. James

Washington, Jr. Now listen, buddy, the paramedics are just downstairs. They'll patch you up good as new, OK? Again, I'm so sorry …'

'You should be!' Leonid said. 'I did not survive in Chechnya to come here for get killed by fucking baby cop, you asshole!'

'Hey, wait a minute …'

But the paramedics were there now, and jostled the rookie out of the way.

'How are you feeling, sir? Describe how you're feeling for me.'

'You are joking, yes? I feel like sack of shit! How I am feeling!'

The paramedics worked on him for a few minutes before getting him up on a stretcher. He heard the word 'stable'. He thought again of that walk with his grandfather, the puzzle he'd been trying so hard for so long to solve, the thing he was being taught but could not remember. It came to him, clearly now: *There was no lesson.* It was just a simple moment of simple chatter while walking in a wood. All that had really happened was that a grandfather had been leading a grandson through a dark yet tranquil part of the forest. And in that memory was everything he'd forgotten that he once knew: the peace we had all known as children. The peace we'd all forgotten.

One of the paramedics leaned in close and said: 'Don't worry.' After what seemed a long pause, he added, earnestly: 'You'll see. You won't die.'

Oh, Leonid had heard this several times before, but always only mockingly, as though he were being challenged to some schoolyard feat of which he was deathly afraid, his peers egging him on. Like climbing up to the highest branch of a tree, when you're scared of heights. Like walking at night through a cemetery amongst the dead, when you're scared of your own mortality. Or like trying to do something as foolish as living in the world when that world and everybody in it scared you worse than death.

NEW FROM PERISCOPE IN 2015

PRINCESS BARI
Hwang Sok-yong; translated from the Korean by Sora Kim-Russell
'The most powerful voice of the novel in Asia today.' (Kenzaburō Ōe)
A young North Korean woman survives unspeakable dangers in
search of a better life in London.
PB • 204MM X 138MM • 9781859641743 • 248PP • £9.99

LONG TIME NO SEE: A MEMOIR OF FATHERS, DAUGHTERS AND GAMES OF CHANCE
Hannah Lowe
'Beautifully woven ... poetically told ... a treasure.' (Kerry Young)
Acclaimed poet Hannah Lowe reflects on her relationship with her
late father, a rakish Jamaican immigrant and legendary gambler.
PB • 204MM X 138MM • 9781859643969 • 328PP • £9.99

THE BLACK COAT
Neamat Imam
'A compelling tale of absurdist humour reminiscent of Bohumil Hrabal.'
(The Independent)
Months after Bangladesh's 1971 war, a simple migrant impersonates
the country's authoritarian ruler – with shocking results.
PB • 204MM X 138MM • 9781859640067 • 352PP • £9.99

THE MOOR'S ACCOUNT
Laila Lalami
'Brilliantly imagined ... feels very like the truth.' (Salman Rushdie)
The fictional memoirs of a Moorish slave offer a new perspective
on a notoriously ill-fated, real-life Spanish expedition in 1528.
PB • 204MM X 138MM • 9781859644270 • 440PP • £9.99

I STARED AT THE NIGHT OF THE CITY
Bakhtiyar Ali; translated from the Kurdish by Kareem Abdulrahman
A group of friends search for the bodies of two murdered lovers in this
haunting allegory of modern Iraqi Kurdistan.
PB • 204MM X 138MM • 9781859641255 • 448PP • £9.99

THE EYE OF THE DAY
Dennison Smith
'Remarkable ... beguiles and enchants on every page.' (Ruth Ozeki)
A privileged boy and a hardened fugitive cross paths mysteriously beginning in
the 1930s, across North America and on the battlefields of wartime Europe.
PB • 204MM X 138MM • 9781859640616 • 328PP • £9.99